Floating unidentified alien cylinders abandoned in space. Shape shifters that can't be killed when they change their forms. Greedy companies that want it all no matter who they have to hurt; it seems that anything can happen in the future.

Brenna and her dad face all of this and more as they chase down the greedy, the thieves, and the kidnappers as part of their job whether they wear spacesuits or run on faraway planets.

Who would guess that the bad guys might be the good ones and the good guys had put a price on their heads. Worst of all, the price for Brenna is her heart.

Bounty On The Beast

ISBN: 978-1-4874-4085-5
Cover art by SudaGraphics Inc

Published by eXtasy Books Inc

Look for us online at:
www.eXtasybooks.com

Bounty On The Beast

By

M. Garnet

CHAPTER ONE

When she was nine, Brenna Gunva shot a reindeer by herself with a bow and arrow, and then finally killed it by slicing its throat. Her father was a harsh teacher who only gave her a nod at her deed.

When she was twelve, her father moved them from Russia to Alaska. She saw no difference in their life as her father continued to force her to live off the land. Coming to the new area, she was tested to learn the tracks of the animals that lived in Alaska. It meant she found a track, followed it to the animal that left the trail and killed that animal. She then matched the paws on the bottom of the dead beast to the prints she had followed and remembered. If possible, they ate the animal. If the animal was inedible, they used it as bait. Nothing was wasted.

Her father taught her the hard way as to how to track across the land that did not accept prints. If she lost a track completely, she got no meal. She learned about bent grass, broken leaves, and bits of fur on briars. There were other lessons, like smells. She had to eat her meals blindfolded and would have items taken away that she couldn't identify from the smell.

As a child, Brenna missed out on a lot of desserts. Her dad would mix fruit on purpose to confuse her nose. He explained that anything she tracked would try to find ways to change or hide their scent to make it hard for a tracker to stay on their trail.

Brenna's father never hit her, but he never saved her from

the injuries she endured during her hunts. The first time a buck speared her with its lowered horns, it took her hours to crawl home. Her father ignored her, as she lay on the floor of their cabin.

Eventually, she got up and took off her clothes to clean up the deep gouge on her ribs. Her dad did give her advice on how to clean the wound and wrap it to help it heal. That was the way it went with each of her injuries, so she learned to avoid lacerations to her body.

Getting hurt while out on a hunt was not the worst part of her solitary life with her father. There was a devil's process created by a twisted mind called Online Schooling. Regardless if her father was home, or on one of his own strange hunts that took him away from her, she had to spend several hours on the computer or doing the assigned homework every day.

There were only two days a year that she was allowed to stay in and rest away from her latest computer or out on a hunt. One was her birthday, and the other was her father's birthday.

From reading and from the computer connected to a satellite, through a special device hidden in a marked tree trunk outside their home, she knew about several other holidays. It seemed that in some parts of the world, businesses also closed and people didn't work on certain holidays. The special holidays were different depending on the country.

Her father insisted her education be broad, so she learned about a lot of religions and what countries they were tied to, and how far back they went in history. Basically, she decided the human race was totally screwed when it came to their beliefs in religions.

Modern politics were learned, with space travel being an important factor, since there were now people who had developed on other worlds. The commonality was that there were many things that she saw in most of them. She saw greed, a divine presence to blame, and a need for power.

The animals she hunted had a better way to handle the situation. They proved that they were the better beast. They didn't use subterfuge, and they didn't lie or set up traps or try bribes. They just proved they were the better beast until a better beast came along to lead the pack.

Seventeen years of harsh living and being brainwashed by a severe father had turned Brenna Gunva into something other than a pretty teen. Her father had created a tracker.

At that age, he took the teen with him on a contract.

Brenna did not understand this country called Texas. The weather was so different from where she had spent her entire life with the need for heavy clothes, it was a surprise to her and was uncomfortable. She would not complain. It was a test.

The one hour trip from Alaska to Texas by air was different than the boat trip from Russia to Alaska, but it still let her know they were going into a different country.

Her Online Schooling gave her credit for being at third level college, so she was well aware of America, and how far it now reached. She also knew that Texas was one of the original 50 states, and had an obnoxious pride in its position.

Keeping her mouth shut and her eyes open, Brenna took in the tall buildings they passed to go out to the dry, hot rolling country.

She listened to the conversation her father had with his employer, while a lot of other armed men stood around a small building. Brenna discovered this was called an outbuilding on a large ranch that belonged to a man who had nothing to do with the problem, or the man that they needed to find in the hills. His location was convenient as he allowed its use by Federal Police.

Listening to the conversation, she learned it was about a man up in the hot, dry hills that had been able to allude all attempts to find him for over two years. There was a large amount of funds that was to be paid to Hian Gunva and his assistant, if he is able to bring in the fugitive, dead or alive.

It took both of them two days to get above the mess left by the many Feds, police, deputies, and local trackers before they got to clean ground to find true tracks. They knew they were finally in the hunting grounds when they began to find recent animal marks.

At dawn, Brenna rolled over to hear the roar in the distance of a rocket taking off for space at the Texas Space Port. She knew from reading that the ships carrying people made a slower and quieter ascent, so this one must be an unmanned vehicle sending up supplies. She looked across a wide dip at a beautiful alpha wolf, staring up and then across to meet her eyes.

Whispering, she spoke to him. "I am sorry we disturb your land." She ducked her head to show submission and waited a moment, even though they were a long distance apart. Brenna had respect for all of Mother Earth's people.

After her younger learning sessions with her father, she never killed what she couldn't eat.

Wolves were not good to eat, but she had shared a meal or two with them.

She pulled out a dried piece of beef to eat for breakfast. She would finish it with water, as she walked. Her father was about a mile west of her. They both were looking for signs. They had a grid worked out in their heads and were working the area to find a trace of this man who had been born in this area. The fugitive knew this land as well as the animals because he had been born and raised in these badlands.

Chapter Two

Brenna built a fire in their cabin in Alaska. She wanted to get rid of the damp cold in the unused home that had settled in while they were gone.

It had taken them a full week, seven days, to find the fugitive. The adversary was smart in that he hadn't built a cabin. That was what the others had looked for, by air and on foot. They would waste days and weeks, encircling every run down shack that hung to the sides of the different low hills.

The fugitive had stashes. Like the animals, he lived off the land and moved from location to location. But like animals, he left spoor. As a higher animal, he buried his shit, but he still pissed standing up, and his markings made animals avoid his area. It was what tipped off Brenna to his trail, and her father followed her as they slowly moved in on him with tranqs.

So they tied him up, built a sled and dragged him down to an area where their mics worked.

From then on she went with her father to fill his contracts. The ones she hated the most were the contracts where they had to retrieve someone from within a city. The smells were difficult, and her clothes had to change to fit into the styles. She was also uncomfortable with how the men looked at her in the skirts or tight slacks.

She knew about sex and had done her own experiments. She read books, saw things on the computer, and decided to try out the process with local boys who were smiling through the whole thing. She found she got better results from her own hand. After all, her lifestyle didn't leave much time for friends. It was hard to have a social life while tearing down an automatic pulse rifle and putting it back together with a blindfold over her eyes.

When she had the weapon back together, her father removed the cloth from around her eyes and sat down across from her at the table.

"I have an offer of a new contract."

She was surprised that he shared this with her. All her life with him he only shared fighting techniques, weapons and ways to live off the land. He taught her in a harsh manner without ever giving her praise. His love or commendations were to share his cabin and his food. Her punishment was the pain of injuries in the field. She knew no other life except that of a tracker.

"When do you leave?"

Her father looked at her as she asked the question. She was surprised as he gave her different information.

"We are going. It is on a moon, not ours. It is a moon with an atmosphere. But we will need off ship suits and some substantial equipment plus pay for some transportation that might be outside the contract."

Thinking for a moment, Brenna looked down at the rifle on the table. "That sounds like a lot of upfront funds."

Her dad went and got his thick metal cased computer with the contact mode that connected directly to above satellites. He enacted it and the holo floating screen popped up in the air between the two of them.

"Brenna, I think it is time I put you into our finance system so that you have access to our funds. Put your left eye right here." He held out a small standard scanner, and she put her open green eye in the proper place. She blinked from the instant flash and her father pulled it back.

Putting things away her father began to talk: "You can now

access any of our accounts from anywhere. In case you are wondering, based on the level of most people in America, we are very wealthy. I have always charged a high fee for the contracts I take on. I always perform as agreed, so the funds pile up. Some seemed to be investments in things I understood, like the company that developed that rifle.

There are whispers that there is a development checkpoint of that rifle which allows it to shoot from mind control. If they get it fully operational, it will put the Space Marine Corps as one of the strongest military units in our section of the universe. The stock in the company will also be important."

Brenna sat with her hands flat on the table and her mouth open. Her father had never shared anything with her. He had always just told her what to do. Perhaps it was the fact that her next birthday was coming up, and she was going to be twenty-two. She didn't think that this age had any particular significance, but everything had changed years ago when she first went to Texas on a Contract Retrieval.

Ever since then she had accompanied her father on each of his contracts all over the world. She studied and learned the real world that she had read or seen on her computer. After each job, they returned to Alaska and both of them went on their own hunts and fishing expeditions.

Her father's voice was low. "Are you wondering why we live so frugal?"

Thinking about his question, she wasn't wondering about their lifestyle. She was wondering what people did with a lot of money. She cleared her throat and spoke as his trained daughter. "So we have enough money to buy the right supplies. I hope the contract is negotiated for a large price. When do we leave?"

The fact that this was her first trip off world with her father to find a fugitive was exciting. He had taken her with him to capture or kill many contracts on Earth. Eventually he had even allowed her to go after some on her own. But now he was taking her out on her first tracker job with him that was somewhere in the known universe.

Their first stop was an outfitter in Detroit, Michigan. The old airport located there was now for raising the ships that took passengers up to grab ships or other places. This was also a place that Hian Gunva had the knowledge of an outfitter who could supply them with what he determined was top line equipment.

Surprised that she found enjoyment in buying things, Brenna wandered down the aisles and added a couple of new knives to her collection. In all the weapons she was proficient in, the knife was her favorite choice. Brenna understood the silence of the knife and knew it was personal.

Upon passing through the loading check point, they were forced to put their weapons into provided large lock boxes that would accompany them. The explanation was that no one except the MPs could travel with weapons on the up-ships or on the grab ships.

Brenna put all her long rifles and guns into the box and when a beep indicated she still had weapons, she put eleven knives from different areas of her uniform and body into the lock box. Evidently the scanner missed the obsidian and glass knives that she could hide easily inside her clothes.

Her studies had let her find that the ancient South American Indians used obsidian for knives and spear and arrow points. It was so strong that it had to be heated as it was chipped and shaped. She had also discovered how small glass knives could be poured and heated over and over to give them strength. She had lost dozens before producing a perfect blue knife that would cut a hair.

Speaking of hair, Brenna braided her long hair and twisted it into a knot at the back of her neck. Having not seen any girl or woman with their hair cut short until she was nine or ten, she just accepted that a long braid was what she should wear. Brenna had a floppy hat that she pulled down low over her green eyes.

She didn't have to hide her smile about her knives as she very rarely smiled. Over the years of her dad's training, he had shown her how the expressions of the face could be read and would tell a whole story about a person.

She had to wonder what weapons her father had on his body as he moved forward to take a seat after being scanned. She sat in the seat behind him so she could look out the window. The long runways that had at one time been the landing and takeoff zones for heavy air containers that people of earth used to travel from one point to another were no longer used as such.

Now, eighty percent of the long strips of cement were a storage area. Local air transport along with space transport units that had to take off and land went straight up or down. It was gravity repulsion.

As they rose in the air, through the window, she saw a group of antique jet planes, rusting on the end of one of the cement strips. Brenna couldn't help but think what a rush it would be to fly one of those slow metal wings through the air of Earth.

Suddenly, the transport kicked in its top drive and they were up into black space. There was no chance to see any views of Detroit or Michigan or even Alaska. Yes, Brenna thought to herself, there might be some things lost with the speed that progress had brought.

At least they didn't have to sit in these tight quarters too long as they met a large grabber ship for their trip to a distant moon. Brenna was now thankful for progress as this meant that the grabber ship would have them at the desired moon without her checking her wrist clock. It was an expensive embedded time and relay piece that would allow her to get a lot of additional information.

It also connected to her floating earplug that let her hear music, news, and talk to her father. Brenna's earplug was even better than the military since she could listen into distance conversations. She was ready for a hunt as she had been trained all her life.

Chapter Three

For eons, the people of Veld had made a decision to protect the world they lived on and enjoyed its benefits. It had two moons and two suns. One moon and one sun that was so far away not to be seen by the naked eye, but still they affected the strong planet.

In the strange way of the fates, there are two large oceans that wrap around and meet at the southernmost points where permanent ice floated in deep concentrations.

The pull of the two moons, one close that lit up the night and one so far away as a bright star, caused a strange atmosphere that left half of the planet desert and, the other half was a dark, damp jungle.

Somewhere in a time too long ago to remember, the people of this planet decided it was beautiful just the way it was, and they would find a way to evolve and grow and become educated without changing or defacing Veld.

So they grew and became part of the jungle and traveled over the desert. They built their homes and schools and later larger science centers in such a way as to not disturb the face of the planet.

They developed and advanced and lived with their world. Somewhere they were granted a small group of shifters. Up to this present time with visitors from other worlds, they still had some traditions that they participated in, especially with their youths.

Before they had the need to construct too many homes and large buildings, they decided to take charge of their population growth. They knew this was one way to protect their world. They didn't condone birth control in the act of destroying a child that had already been conceived; they worked on ways to prevent conception until the thought was complete between both parties.

Once other worlds discovered them, it was found that what looked like uncouth jungle natives turned out to be scientists far ahead in matters of controlling the mind and body.

The children from age four to ten were in a harsh school of nature learning the ways of the desert and the jungle. To outsiders this looked a bit harsh and depending on the age and size and ability of the child, they spent time in very unusual degrees of introduction to the wildlife of their planet. They were inducted into various degrees of tests both naked in the desert and the jungle.

They soon learned what could kill them in both sections of their world and what they might find to survive and live. Each test, as they got older became longer and more dangerous, but all of the children that were submitted always survived.

By the age of ten, there were some decisions made, as among the young and from that time forward they seemed to find a direction for their future. No one forced the young ones to stay on a straight path, but no one was surprised when a budding mathematician or physician continued to prove that the beginning happened at ten years of age in the jungle.

There was one strange power that came out between nine and ten and stayed all their lives. It was rare as only a few in each age group had the right unusual genes to become modifiers.

For these rare ones, the tests would continue. They had to learn life and control. They would know pain and torture and the hurt of being alone. It is their thought that the planet gave the people a gift for protecting it, warriors that could fight anyone that came to harm them or their world.

But besides the normal education that a growing boy would need, and the modifiers were always male, they needed to understand their world and their bodies and control. So, they were taught everything about Veld and—added to this—they were instructed about the worlds in this sector of the universe that held life that would interact with them.

The important and worst part of the modifier's life was the act of learning control. They could not turn into the huge warrior just because a school friend tripped them on a jungle path. So, the elders put them through pain and insults and anger. The teachers for the young with this talent were adult modifiers who could tear a forty-foot tree from the ground with one hand before they shifted.

They made life miserable for these young men, as they knew the dangers involved in having such talents. These few young boys had better senses even in their standard form than the average person on Veld.

Their eyesight lets them see in the darkness, their smell both through their nose and mouth were those of the large Calluf cat. The Calluf was the most dangerous animal in the jungles of Veld, as it grew to over four hundred pounds and had long teeth left over from prehistoric times. What it hunted it found to kill and eat.

In their modified form, even a young boy could repel the attack from such an animal as their body picked up the strength from the Mother Earth and some thought this was from some metals. It was proven that in their modified form they deflected modern bullets and turned phaser weapons back on the shooters.

There were many discussions among the scientists and elders on this world as if the modifiers had evolved to handle the modern weapons or had always been such strong beasts. The warriors had their own armor within the cells of their bodies. The only thing they all agreed about was that these warriors were their blessing.

There was never a war within the people of Veld. There were yearly challenges among the warriors that represented districts. In ancient times, it settled dangerous disputes. In modern times, it is a great entertainment and with much funds changing hands.

During Zander's father's lifetime, people from other worlds landed on Veld. The elders and scientists were not surprised, as they had been studying the universe for some time. They saw the ships moving from point to point and even knew the original locations of some of them.

They were attacked by a greedy race originally from the planet Wisoosio. The Wisoo people were similar to the Veldans as were most people in the universe. Nature seemed to find a design that worked and stayed with it.

The Wisoosio had spread out through many planets, conquering and claiming, but they found resistance on Veld. They found warriors they couldn't conquer and a people they couldn't control. It was a rich planet they wanted, but the price was proving too great until they decided that the warriors themselves were of interest.

Military who originally came from a planet called Earth offered assistance, and the elders agreed to a joint covenant. In time, the Wisoo invaders were beaten back and became only a small irritation as they tried to kidnap a modifier now and then at a great deal of damage and expense to their own people.

Time passed, and the friendship between the Veldans and the military from Earth grew. The Earth military often requested to have one of the modifiers accompany them on rescue missions against Wisoo or other dangerous incidents.

Zander's life as a modifier meant he spent his early life divided between living rough in the jungle, being hunted by adult modifiers who beat him if they caught him, and then . . . hurt or not . . . spending hours in school. He grew up as he was supposed to, a tough warrior. He proved the training was what produced a good modifier who could control his talents.

Zander turned out better. He claimed the jungle talked to him, and the elders believed him. So it was no surprise that he was in the jungle when the call was sent to him that he was needed for an assignment. It might have surprised the elders to know who his companion was in that tall tree.

He scratched the ears of the large cat known as a Calluf before he left the dangerous killer in the tree and dropped down to go back to his home. He was soon ready for whatever assignment his elders had for him to attend.

Chapter Four

Brenna and her father were going through their storage locker in Anchorage. They paid a premium for this unit, as the entire multi units were fire protected and set up inside an old military warehouse.

The owners had discovered that many wealthy hunters from the lower states were willing to pay premium rates to ensure that their storage units had the best protection from a careless neighbor. Besides the protected walls and fireproof insulation, Hian had added a state of the art alarm system that included a camera in all corners and a heat seeker disabler. The disabler would shoot and put several invaders asleep.

The unit was full of composite storage boxes in various colors and some in heavy duty carry cases to protect the contents. All explosives were also in containment cases. There was a pull- down shelf that they could use as a desk just inside the door. It was here that Brenna and her dad would sometimes look over the list of items in the storage or discuss a new contract.

Hian spread out some papers and looked at his daughter. He was very proud of this woman but had never found the words to tell her his feelings. He was just a man of action after his heart was gone with the death of Brenna's mother.

"Brenna, we have a nice problem."

Brenna was straightening some of the smaller plastic boxes on top of weapons cases. "What do you have?"

"We have been offered two large contracts."

Turning, Brenna saw the new papers that were spread out

on the desk. "Tell me the short story on both."

Putting the papers into two piles, her father pointed at one as he spoke. "An insane megalomaniac has kidnapped a child of one of the senators of the General Earth Government. He has taken the twelve-year-old to the mines on Mars and has already blown up several above site centers, killing over twenty civilians."

Leaning her hip against a stack of containers, she needed more information. "So, how dangerous do they think the pervert is right now?"

Hian picked up a tab and inserted it into his reader. A holo came up to float above the desk. "He wiped out a small marine unit that was sent in to retrieve him. Now I understand why they are offering so much for his retrieval, alive or dead. They do want the girl alive."

"How much is the contract?"

Pointing with his finger as he read aloud from the screen. "One million creds."

Brenna whistles. "So, they have a track on the girl and know she is still alive." She was just thinking aloud. That was a lot of money.

"What is the second contract?" She looked at the second stack of papers.

"A man attached to a group of Space Marine Corps unit on protection duty for some scientists who are examining a new find. He stole an artifact, took a small jump ship and crashed on an uninhabited planet. The marines refuse to go after him. They are offering one point five million creds."

At hearing that large amount, Brenna couldn't even whistle. The large amount was offered only to them, and it was larger than anything that they had seen in contracts before as they tracked for credits.

"Why so much for that man and why won't the Marines go after him? Change the tabs so you can show me the information on the second contract."

"Hmm." Her dad's finger changed pages. "The planet he landed on is still in an early stage of development. There are lots of volcano's and big reptiles that are equal to T-Rex and Raptors. But the most important issue is that this guy is from the planet U231Z42 or known by the native population as Veld. Within its population are a few individuals called modifiers. We call them shape shifters. They can turn into large beasts with their intelligence still intact, and they are almost indestructible.

They have helped protect the Marines in certain situations. That is probably why the Marines aren't willing to hunt him. I also think the Marines are smart enough to know how dangerous he is and don't want to face him just to get back some old gadget he has taken."

Hian pulled the tab and shut down the reader. "So on one we have no air and on the other we have reptiles that want to eat us, interesting locations for trackers."

She nodded. "But both places leave tracks. Hey, remember when you were telling me about your dream of having a company and being a boss and going semi-retired? Two point five creds with what we have in various accounts would probably get us there."

"There is a satellite that they have closed down that is for sale. There are a lot of badass wannabe trackers out there just waiting for some training and to be put to work. We already have the reputation for being good on contracts to keep us going." He stopped talking and shuffled the papers.

"Dad, do you mean you would move away from Earth?"

"We have learned all we can on this old world. We need to teach ourselves what is out there." He waved his hand upward at the metal insulated ceiling.

She stood up and smiled. "So, let's take them both. You can take Mars, as you do well in the new space suits. I will go to the planet with big geckos because I am too small to even be an appetizer to them."

Ever since that first tracker contract a couple of years ago, when he had taken her with him off Earth, they had traveled together, often to far away places in the known universe. She smiled at the thought that Bad Guys were everywhere humans had settled, on planets or moons and even satellites.

It took her two days to convince him to take both contracts. It was another Earth week to work out the details of the wording in the contracts and the terms of the payments.

At last, it was time to go to their favorite outfitter in Detroit and buy the best equipment available for two different types of worlds. The outfitter never revealed how he was able to offer the latest equipment and military weapons, but Hian trusted what he purchased and never argued price.

The owner was always happy to see him and preferred to take both of them into the back area of his warehouse where new ships with the military labels were still attached to boxes. There the Gunvas filled their lists.

Among all the usual things like new weapons and resistant clothes, Hian needed heat seekers that could tell the difference between the adult and the child. He added a thermal atmosphere pouch as it was his intention to track and kill the idiot and capture and retrieve the child.

He added three off ship suits to make sure he had backups. He needed hard weapons that fired better without atmosphere instead of phasers, but he still added a couple of hand phase guns.

For Brenna, she needed grenade launchers, portable nets, and stun guns. These were handheld weapons that could kill T-Rex. She wanted to capture the Veldan and get the artifact so she could return both of them to the Marines.

Father and daughter needed long distance communication devices of various types. All of it was chosen to be lightweight so that they could carry what they needed with them and travel as fast as they could on their own feet.

Finally, they were ready, and both went up on the same ship but separated on their out rides. Hian could take a local jump ship to Mars, but Brenna had to take a bigger grab ship to an outer location near the planet where her mark had crashed.

The big grab ship made her trip hardly any longer than her dad's trip to Mars. The grab ship got its name from the strange motor that reaches out into space and found the magnetic threads that crisscrossed space. When the pilot found the one he wanted, the strange motor grabbed the string and wham; they were in another part of this sector of the universe.

The longest part of the grab ship travel was the wait for the pilot to find the line he needed. Brenna spent this time studying her target. The man seemed to be a hero on his home world. He had done several military stints with the Marines when they were fighting what the Marines called Trio on a couple of planets. He was big, seven feet tall in his normal mode as a man.

It seemed he could shift into something indestructible, called a modifier that could be as tall as nine feet and wide enough to turn sideways to go through Earth-size doors.

His government had accepted a request to supply one of the modifiers along with the Space Marine Corps units that were going into an alien container that had been discovered drifting in space.

The owners or builders of the container were unknown, but it seemed to have been used to collect items and animals for the owners. Something had gone wrong and many of the dangerous animals had gotten loose and killed off anything and anyone with whom they came into contact.

To make matters more interesting, there were killer robots on the container that tried to eliminate anything. Scientists going into the container needed lots of protection.

According to the report that was turned in, the latest insertion group had discovered a room with artifacts. It seemed there was a small item that the Veldan was immediately drawn to, and he picked it up and put it inside his jacket.

Scientists immediately began to complain and told him all items belonged to them until identified and classified. He said the item was an ancient artifact from his world, and he was taking it home.

There was a demand for the return of the item without a description. The Veldan returned to the skip ship and everyone waited for decisions from the officials from SMC and Veld.

Veld indicated they wanted to see the artifact and Earth replied it could not be moved until it was in the hands of the scientists first and identified and classified. It then would be turned over to the Marines and Veld could make a claim to prove that the artifact might be something from their history.

Brenna decided that the modifier took things into his own hands and threw the pilot and co- pilot into the tube connecting the skip ship to the container. He disconnected everything and took off.

It took the Marines twenty-four hours to trace where the skip ship had been crashed on the uninhabited planet. It was assumed the Veldan remained on the planet with the unknown artifact. Her arrangements were to be taken to the planet in a skip ship and dropped near the crash site in a single person pod. From there she was on her own.

Chapter Five

Zander liked this forest. It wasn't the deep wet jungle he had been raised in, but it was full of life and lots of food. Even the large ferns had edible parts to them and nuts and fruit fell from the tall trees.

He ate the meat raw, too smart to build fires. After crashing the jump ship, he had taken the time to destroy it enough so that it would never fly again. He knew that if he got off this planet, it wouldn't be on that ship; it would be with help sent from his home world.

He had felt the draw of the artifact and knew that his elders would eventually want it on the land where it had been created back in history. It was special, and he would keep it protected from foreign eyes.

Every day he put more distance between himself and the crash site. The days were only a bit shorter than those on Veld, and he had begun to shut his internal clock down to adjust to this planet's day and night cycle.

Right now he was having fun following an extremely large animal. He had discovered from watching it that it was a vegetarian, and its long body let it eat from the tall trees. Its wide tail and flat feet were making a perfect path for him that hid his marks. Fortunately, it was lumbering in the direction he needed to travel.

One thing he found in abundance was eggs. He needed to find a hot spring off of one of the volcanos so that he could cook eggs and fish, but he had to wait for one to be in the direction he was heading.

He had only had to modify once, and it was his fault. He had misjudged an animal that was about his size that was also eating someone's eggs. His intent was to allow it to eat along with him. There were several nests with eggs the size of his head nestled in leaves.

It seemed the reptile didn't want to share and as Zander had his back bent he felt the curved claw rake deep into his hips. Instinctively he changed into a beast that could accept and fight off the long mouth full of teeth. He tore away the short front arms full of the curved claws and kicked back at the rear feet that were kicking at him.

In this stronger mode, he continued to tear the reptile apart and stopped when he had a haunch to eat, and he lumbered away. With a full belly and finding a stream, the beast in him was finally beginning to settle down. As he returned to a man, he waded into the water and washed away the aftermath of the fight.

He was careful not to underestimate the size of the small brains and bodies of the animals that roved this forest. The Mother Earth who watched over the growth and development of this planet allowed for all life to be smart. Maybe their brains were still small, but their instincts were strong.

Both Zander and several reptiles looked up at the sound in the sky as he saw a single person pod travel down towards the forest.

Fuck, I have a visitor.

He had enjoyed having the world just to himself. It reminded him when he was a boy, and he had been taken into the jungle to learn to live on his own. This time with the wild reptiles and the large ferns and tall trees had brought him closer to his ancestors than he had been since that childhood time.

He was a distance from the crash site on purpose, but maybe it would be better to know the enemy.

Brenna had very little control over the small pod, but she was able to bring it down through the tall trees and crash through the underbrush to stop on its back. She waited a few long minutes before popping the top hinge open.

Knowing the noise as the pod came in through the atmosphere was enough to wake up anything for miles, she knew her approach was announced.

Getting out, she immediately grabbed her weapons and slung her pack over her shoulder. She had her thirteen knives, including the hidden ones and she brought out her special scanner. She hoped it could tell the difference between reptiles and a shape shifter. She had been told that some of the animals looked like reptiles but were warm-blooded.

It was the beginning of the development of the future of this world, but it could screw up her modern tech equipment. Brenna was glad she had her old-fashioned tech to fall back on as she looked at the footprints around her in the bent grass.

She listened as the world came back alive after the silence her entrance had caused. Slowly, birds began to call, tree animals began to move, and ground reptiles looked around for their quest. Even with a loud noise, life goes on, and hunger must be sated.

The heavy weapon Brenna slung across her chest was to make sure she wasn't something's dinner. She had a bunch of portable nets in her different pockets to catch the special beast that was on this planet. The one that when she caught him, she would radio up for a pick up from the skip ship that was circling above.

This was a large area to search, yet she had a starting point. He also had crashed in this forest on purpose. So he had gotten things to survive out of the skip ship and started out into the forest. Being part of the universal human race he had probably headed for water even though there would have been some portables in the ship.

It took her a careful hour to get to the ship. She was right in her assessment; the crash had been deliberate and without much damage.

She waited another hour watching small animals go in and out of the open hatch. Deciding it was empty of anything large and dangerous she carefully entered herself and had a shock. There were things still inside that she thought a man in a forest alone would have taken with him.

There were weapons in their bolted locations. There were waterproof ponchos and flares and even a scanner that had fallen beneath the front console. The man who had stolen a very important artifact had taken it and nothing else to go out into a very dangerous forest.

Brenna had gone over the information given to her and nowhere was there a description of the artifact. She wondered if the artifact was small enough to be swallowed by a reptile when it ate the man who crashed this small ship. The result would mean that the artifact would then be deposited miles away in the spoor of that reptile.

Maybe the artifact was large, and that was why he couldn't carry anything but a heavy, bulky item. So there was a tall man from the planet Veld out in this forest lugging around a heavy ancient something. Brenna decided that picture just didn't make sense, especially as she went back outside to look at old footprints.

This man did not make deep footprints. She knew he was about seven feet tall and should weigh two hundred pounds of tight muscle. Even without a heavy load, he should leave deep marks, but this man walked light on the ball of his foot. Not only that, within a few yards he found hard ground and rocks and timber. His marks on the ground began to disappear. She was tracking a man who was used to the forest and didn't need the trappings from the ship to live off the land.

That was why she was here. She knew what it was like to live off the land, even a new forest with reptiles. If he hadn't left footprints, the hungry animal that got his smell left plenty. A large reptile that walked upright and tipped back now and then on its tail was following a warm- blooded two-footed dinner.

For a full day, she took her time following the old trail, once in a rare moment finding a print of a shoe. Brenna decided he was moving away from the crash site. It is something she would have done to escape the Marines when they came down for him. Except the Marines didn't want to face T-Rex.

That night she shimmied up a tree far from where she peed and tied her body in the crotch of a limb. She ate protein and drank water with a couple of recommended pills for the biting insects. She set up a very tight movement alarm and allowed herself to sleep.

Brenna woke before dawn to a couple of large reptiles eating a cat that had tried to climb the tree to get to her location. She ate an egg log and waited for the guys at the bottom to get bored and hungry enough to move on to easier meals.

The sun was up, but it was only thin strips that could drift through the heavy tops of the thick trees covered in vines. On the ground, there were more ferns, more giant ferns than there was brush.

The third day she found where he had buried his tracks by following a mammoth reptile that left a trail that was several yards wide. She only found his boot print twice, and both were partials when he slid off rocks.

Brenna had to smile because he was really good. It was like he knew someone would be coming to track him. She wondered if he had played this game before in his life. Had he been raised like her father had raised her, in the wilds with animals?

Chapter Six

Zander changed his direction to circle around to find out who might be trying to find him. He knew it was only one person, so the Marines had not come down in force after him and the artifact.

He also thought that his home world was delaying diplomatic talks on the return of the artifact. He had not been able to let his people know what he had found, but he had no doubt that it belonged on his world.

He would not turn it over to a full team of Marines or one tracker, no matter what type of weapons that tracker carried. He had to wonder how much was offered to an off-worlder, in order to get him to come to a planet full of dinosaurs, to capture an angry modifier that even frightened the Wisoo.

Not wanting to cross over his trail, he moved around, taking his time to get into a position to watch the tracker. After a day and night, he saw the small person dressed in tight clothes of dark green mottled with black from head to toe. The clothing was a smart choice, as nothing hooked or stuck to it as the figure moved through the ferns and tall grasses.

He knelt down on a heel as he watched the movements of the small figure. This one was smart, moving slowly and often stopping to look and listen. Also, this tracker wasn't leaving much in the way of a trail.

An uncomfortable feeling went down Zander's spine. This tracker was too good. There was a story here that could cause him real problems. He made a quick decision that had a lot to do with protecting the artifact. He was going to send the tracker back home empty-handed.

Spending another night up a tree was beginning to be a habit for Brenna. This time, she wasn't bothered by any animals below, but she did have to share the limb with a small snake who appreciated her body warmth.

Moving slowly, she unwrapped the snake peacefully as she let it move out on the limb. She had learned at an early age that it wasn't the size of the snake that indicated their danger. She untied her rope and, as quiet as possible, lowered down to the ferns below.

She got rid of her bodily functions and then drank the last of her bottled water, putting the empty container inside her backpack. Other than her body discharges, that she covered, she never left debris anywhere, especially on a pristine planet like this forested world.

She checked her equipment as she looked around to make sure there wasn't anything close that wanted a snack, and then began to try and pick up the trail again.

Recognizing that she was still on an old trail, her hopes were that it would lead her to a closer trail or a place where he stopped.

Suddenly, she stopped and knelt down in the shelter of some large ferns. She saw a fresh partial boot print that crossed the path in front of her. A single piece of grass was disturbed, but nothing else showed that anyone or any animal had passed in that direction.

Where was he going and where had he come from, that crossed the trail that he took in a forward point away from the crash site? There was something wrong, as she sat down on her butt under the feathers of the larger ferns. Here the ground was bare and somewhat dry, and she would have to sweep her hand to wipe away the traces of her presence.

She waited and watched a small reptile on four legs move past in a hurry. It went in the same direction of that one print and destroyed a portion of the partial impression. She decided that enough time had gone by and eased out to follow the small four-legged animal.

Something had frightened the reptile, as it was long gone with a speed she didn't want to replicate. She stayed close to the shelter of the ferns, letting them hide her from anything above. At last, the ground seemed to move upward, and she felt the tremors of a volcano in the distance. The volcano didn't worry her, as it was too far away to be any danger, and was just releasing a small amount of gas.

There was no sign in this area of any flows for too long to disturb the growth and the deep loam. Ahead she saw the four-legged animal on a ledge as it leaped off into the forest below.

She looked down to watch where she was placing her feet and froze, as she saw where the reptile had again defaced the edge of a boot impression. Without moving, she raised her head and looked up and around to make sure she was alone. If she went out on that ledge, she would be exposed, as there was no cover except for the rocks at the back.

The hair on her arms inside the tough material tingled in warning, and she felt that this might be a trap. Could a large animal lure its supper here by chasing the smaller short guy ahead and off the end into the trees?

Without turning and with her knees bent she took one step back when she was hit in the back, and a heavy weight pressed her to the rocky ledge, knocking her breath from her chest as her weapon was pressed into her breasts.

A hand reached around her head and turned her face to the side, putting pressure on her neck until she couldn't pull air into her lungs. She fought by kicking and bucking and pounding her fists, but the weight on her was too heavy, and the turn of her neck was consistent. She felt the blackness behind her eyes as she scraped through her gloves at the rock. Then it was over as, without air, she fell into darkness.

Zander wasn't sure what shocked him the most, that she was a woman, or that she was such a good tracker, or that she had so many knives on her person.

She had fought like a Bensail cat from his world. His much greater weight and the larger size was an obvious decision of the outcome of the battle from the first, even without his beast coming forward.

He had assumed it was a small male tracker they had hired from some mercenary world to come after him and the artifact. But when the unconscious body was flipped over, he pulled the head cover off to discover the unusual shape of a woman . . . who had a very long braid of dark hair that laid across the rock.

He began to remove her things, building a pile at one side that grew to an alarming size. Her front rifle and the backpack were expected, and the hand weapon strapped to her hip was not too much of a surprise. But in her pockets, as he removed her jacket he found fifteen grenades and a pound of soft explosive.

He weighed the explosive, wondering what the hell she was planning to blow up with all that power. Pulling her boots off he found a nice knife and set it aside. Her pants came off next, leaving her in the neck-to-ankles two-piece soft snug garment that must be meant to protect her body from the harsher outer suit.

In her pants, he found what she meant for him, dozens of portable nets. One or two of these nets would contain him in his normal state. None of them would contain him in his modified mode, but there were few that understood the strength and what the beast could use from the earth and metal and power, to escape confinement.

He found several more knives in the pants. This female tracker must like the sharp instruments. He turned her over and began to pat down her back. She was a lot of muscle with some soft spots that were in the right places. Maybe he had been alone too long, as he was inspecting some dimples in her ass and found a knife tucked between her cheeks.

He looked at it in the light and realized this small sharp blade was glass. Amazing. He laid it by the others, a group of amazing cutting tools.

He flipped her back over onto her back and found pleasure in checking her breasts. Sure enough, there was one more hidden weapon just below and almost between her mounds. Reaching under her shirt, he pulled out the small black knife that he knew immediately was made of some type of Mother Earth product.

Okay, he would leave her one knife and enough shots in the rifle to protect herself. He went through her backpack and pulled out her contact unit for the skip ship that would retrieve her when she called. He moved the pile over several yards to the edge of the rocky shelf and moved a couple of large stones in front of the pile.

He used her explosives and blew it all up. The loud noise shook the ground, and he heard her moan as her lungs filled with clean air.

He stood watching her and fired the rifle until the load level read that it was only at an eighth full.

Brenna slowly rose up and breathed through her sore throat. She tried her voice. "Are you going to kill me?"

"No. I am leaving you enough firepower to protect yourself until your ride picks you up. I have destroyed all your other weapons, well most of them." He knelt down on a heel and looked at her.

"What is this made of?" He was holding her obsidian knife. A reflex made her grab for her breast. "You stripped me?"

He shook his head with a small smile. "I didn't remove your under clothes. What is this made from?"

Brenna looked at the man who was holding one of her favorite toys. He was large, but all of his proportions were well developed, and nothing was unusual. She decided he was handsome, in a rough way with blue, green eyes and brown hair that touched his shoulders.

The look he was giving her with his thick eyebrows raised didn't seem that threatening. Still, he had laid out a trap for her, taken her down without a sound, and left her unconscious while he took all of her weapons.

For such a calm man, she knew the hand holding her toy was very dangerous. He waited for her to answer about the small knife he was holding.

She sighed and pulled her knees up to her chest. "It is called obsidian. Some think it is made from a type of rock or glass from a volcano."

He flipped it a couple of times in his one hand, catching both the handle and the pointed end.

Okay, he knew knives.

She shifted and found that her glass toy was also missing. Zander was meticulous in his search of her body, even though her body suit was still in place. Looking around she saw the stack of her knives with the shine of the small glass one reflecting the leaves of the trees above. She felt her anger growing, despite what her father had taught her about control. The hunted had turned into the hunter. Shit.

Looking around she saw the streaks of black where he had blown up a lot of rocks and part of the ledge, making the area smaller.

With a snippy voice, she asked her next question. "So, what happens now?"

He stood up and walked over to her rifle and nudged it with his foot. She looked up at his entire height. He would make a great player in the old basketball game, as he had to be at least seven feet tall. How had such a big man been able to move through the forest so quietly?

"You have only a small load left in this weapon. I will allow you one knife and your call unit so you can notify the skip ship up there to come and retrieve you. You will be safe enough until they retrieve you. Don't come back."

He picked up the group of knives and started to pull out a good silver one, but she stopped him. "I want the obsidian knife."

He gave her a long look then shook his head. "It is a knife belonging to Mother Earth. Choose another."

Brenna let out a huff with her words. "I'll take the silver knife."

He dropped the silver knife by her bare feet and before she could even reach for it, he was gone, over the edge and into the forest.

Damn, damn, damn. Curse words were all that came out with the anger inside her head. She jumped up and tried to get to the edge to see where he went. She limped, as she stepped on a small sharp rock. At the edge, she looked at the tops of smaller trees and tall ferns. Nothing was moving. He had blended into the forest as if he were a part of what nature produced on this planet.

She did see movement off in the distance, but as she watched, she recognized the heads of the tall reptiles that ate the leaves as they moved. She found some more words that her father would disapprove of and limped back to the contact unit.

Chapter Seven

Brenna did not ask for retrieval; she asked for an equipment pod to her location. She had three identical pods on the skip ship with everything she needed to be a tracker on this planet. Her dad had taught her to have backups.

Too bad the pilot didn't have. Still, she kept her eyes on the site as the pod landed several yards away. It meant that almost naked, almost without good weapons, she had to climb off the ledge and walk barefoot through the forest to find the equipment pod.

The first animal that picked up her scent took most of the charge left in her weapon. It wasn't that big, but it was strong with a large mouth full of teeth and curved claws on all four feet. She managed to stay out of its reach, barely.

Without any shoes and one foot cut from a sharp rock, she wasn't exactly fast in her movements. She had marked the spot the equipment pod had landed from up on the ledge, but limping through giant ferns with the cover of the heavy trees it was difficult to find the site.

At last, she looked up and saw the broken limbs that showed the entrance of the pod as it crashed down through the planet's growth. The noise had chased everything away, so there weren't any threats by any reptiles as she stumbled through the path of broken and bent foliage to get to the pod.

Sitting down with her legs spread she popped open the pod and smiled. For a tracker like her, this was Christmas. Before she began to put on her clothes, she pulled out a bottle of water. She took a long drink and found a towel to wipe her feet. She put a bandage on the cut on one and then began to dress in the strong resistant tight uniform.

She couldn't find a comb, but she unbraided her tossed hair and re-braided it as tight as she could so that she could put it up under her face and head cover. She pulled out the empty backpack and began to fill it as well as the pockets on her uniform. There was a fully charged pulse rifle, a pistol on her hip, and the portal nets.

She looked at the explosives and left them. They were useless against someone who moved too fast and didn't make a nest or stay in a cave. She didn't need any extra weight as she tracked this strange man through this forest.

At last Brenna felt she was ready. She knew he had a head start, but she was a trained tracker, the best next to her father. She would find him again and this time, he would not surprise her. She set the pod to destroy itself in ten minutes.

She was several yards into the ferns and across a small stream when she heard the small sound of the pod explosion. As she walked, she found some young trees and she pulled leaves to rub on her suit and shoes to cover her scent. She wasn't sure if the man could smell her but she knew the reptiles could, and she didn't need to be sidetracked to fight off some hungry animal.

Zander had heard the pod come in and realized it was not the noise of a skip ship to pick his female tracker up; it was just an unmanned pod dropping down. He stopped and shook his head thinking of her unusual green eyes.

"She is like the Bensail, small and angry for her size," he spoke aloud to himself as he thought of the deadly small cat that lived within the jungle of his home world.

She was the best natural warrior that he had come across that was from another world. He sat up on a tree limb, feeding nuts to a little animal that had adopted him. The adoption probably came because he shared the nuts.

She was moving slowly and quietly, carefully pulling leaves to rub the sap on her to cover her scent. Clever girl. She was back in her suit, covered from head to toe in dark green mottled with black. He watched her stop and stoop over and mess with the ground behind her and cover whatever she was leaving with leaves.

He smiled as he understood she was leaving traps so he couldn't sneak up on her from behind.

She didn't understand how he had found and attacked her the last time. It was from above.

As a precocious child made to live in the jungle, he had taken to the life with pleasure. He had found one of the Bensail kittens whose mother had been killed by off-worlders.

The kit snarled but was starving, and he killed a large bird and shared the meal with the dark animal. From that time on the cat followed him as it grew to be an adult. It would disappear to hunt on its own, sometimes bringing him a share.

If he were sitting on a high rock or a tree limb eating a meal, it would claw up beside him, and he shared. He would scratch under the jaw and at the back where the tail began and the cat purred.

He never named the cat, and it never came near him if there was any other person within sight except for one time. He was in his modified form and fighting off a group of Trios, and suddenly the small deadly cat was at the throat of one of the off-worlders.

The Trio was no match for the teeth and claws of the wild animal and Zander fought harder to destroy the rest and go to help his friend. But the cat had not needed help as it licked blood from its fur as it sat on the chest of a dead Trio.

Eventually, the short life of the Bensail began to show as white hairs began to grow around its face and it ate more meals from Zander's hands. There came a time when Zander went into the jungle, and the cat did not join him. He never saw it again and just assumed it had lost its last battle, dying in honor in a fight. That is the way of the jungle.

He had decided this little tracker would not die in this prehistoric forest. Anyone with her skills and those beautiful green eyes needed to exist in the universe as long as possible.

So he became her guardian, staying in the trees above and watching her fight off the animals. He would go down to take out a couple of dangerous reptiles with small brains and large stomachs that would have taken her out as a pair.

Eventually, she found a trace of him when he was trying to protect her one night. She began to backtrack and set a different type of trap. The traps blew up some animals and she didn't sleep for a couple of nights. She was getting tired and becoming a danger to herself.

As he watched from sitting on comfortable limbs she had been fighting through the ferns and small animals for fourteen days, the last couple without rest. At last, she found the strength to climb a tree near him and tie herself onto a center and instantly fell asleep.

Brenna rolled over to let the heat warm her front now that her back was nice and cozy. It was at that thought that her eyes popped open. Tied to a tree did not produce the warmth of a fire that was in front of her face. Without moving she saw the man sitting across the fire from her, watching her with his strange blue-green eyes. He knew she was awake, but he didn't move and didn't say anything.

Looking down at herself in the firelight, she realized that once again she was in the light underwear and barefoot. She felt her face color in shame. Twice the man she was to retrieve as a tracker had captured her and disarmed her. There was no way that she could ever face her father again.

Hian Gunva was a man born into a world that only allowed the strong to live. He had been born in Norway but had been inducted at an early age as an orphan into a military group used to rescue stranded individuals from totally frozen locations.

Being a small child and youth, he was the brunt of all the jokes by the large Norwegians that thought they were descended from the Vikings. He learned to fight in order to survive, to fight dirty since he was fighting kids and later men who had more muscles than were on his thin body. He shared with his daughter that he found a talent and he studied every written, taped or word on hand to hand fighting. He became an expert and then went onto finding how to track a person. His education was strange and sometimes incomplete, so he made sure that his daughter had an education on a level far above his.

As a teacher he was harsh, and he did not have it in him to show emotions to the female child.

Her father molded her into a tracker supreme and now she had failed. She couldn't return.

Zander watched her across the fire, but there was something different. Where was his wild Bensail? She lay without moving and the beautiful large green eyes filled up with moisture. He didn't think this warrior female was the type to cry.

He kept his voice soft. "Are you injured?"

Her voice was a whisper. "You have killed me."

Zander was sitting on his ass with his knees pulled up and his arms across his knees. He gripped his fingers together and tried to think her words through to their meaning.

"I am not going to hurt or kill you. Like the last time, I will leave you with enough to protect yourself until you call your ship for retrieval." He watched her face as the firelight played across the smooth planes of high cheeks and full lips.

"I can't return." Still her voice was a whisper. Now she closed her eyes and rolled over onto her back.

He looked at the small smoke wisps trailing up into the air.

"What is your name?" He wasn't sure why he wanted to know, but it seemed like a moment to get closer to the human side of him.

She sighed and spoke above a whisper, "I'm Brenna Gunva."

"Hello Brenna, I am Zander. Did they tell you who and what I am when you took this job?" Rolling back over, she looked at the fire as she decided to talk. "I didn't get the first contract.

My father gets the first contacts and all the information. I know that there is a big price on your head and that you are a thief. You stole something important from the Earth Space Marine Corp. They are a very tough and very important group used to keeping security and war problems under control in this sector of the universe."

He picked up a small piece of wood and broke it in half and put both pieces on the fire. "If the Marines are so tough, didn't you think it strange that they didn't send a marine unit after me instead of asking an outside mercenary to take on the job?"

Watching her carefully, Zander knew he was reaching her through her depression. She sat up slowly, pulling her knees tight to her chest and looking up to watch the smoke disappear in the night.

Not wanting to disturb the reptiles any more than he already had, he kept his voice low but enough for her to hear. "I'll ask you again, do you know who and what I am as a warrior from Veld?"

At last Brenna began to think she might live after all. When she first woke up she had decided she would take her life before she would report back to her father that she had failed. This big man was beginning to cut into her need to understand and discover. It was only a different form of tracking.

"Zander, what did you steal?"

She heard a deep chuckle and looked over at him. She had avoided meeting those unusual eyes, but now in the firelight, she decided they must be the color of his home jungle.

"What did you steal?"

"I didn't steal anything. I found and retrieved an ancient artifact that belongs to my people. I intend to return it to my planet and it will be put on display in a very religious place in honor of the Mother planet."

Chapter Eight

Brenna was wondering if there was more to this hunt than she had originally thought when she had talked her father into taking on both contracts. The credits were unusually high, and it would get them into a different type of life as trackers.

Looking at him carefully, this was the first time Brenna had a chance to see the tall man in full detail. She wasn't sure what he had worn when he was with the Marine detail. They were to act as protection for the nosy scientists who wanted something from an unknown alien container full of dangerous animals.

He must have been dressed in the same way to the Marines since he had on pants and boots that looked like marine issue material. On the other hand, living in the forest, it was evident he had adapted his clothes to let his big body be comfortable in the heat and the fact that it rained often.

He had cut off his pants to above the knees, and his shirt had no sleeves, show the tight muscles in the long arms that rested on his knees. The shirt was unbuttoned and showed the dark tanned skin over rows of muscle going down to his belt.

"Zander, you hid or buried the artifact here on this world. If it is that important you won't stay very far from it, so since I can't return as a failure, you can at least tell me what the artifact is and why it is so important to your people?"

He shook his head. "The artifact has to do with what I am. Brenna, I am a modifier warrior. Some of your people call me a shape shifter. The reason the Marines didn't come for me is that in my modified form, the Marines can't take me prisoner, and I can destroy an entire unit within minutes."

Shaking her head, Brenna tried to digest his words.

Zander continued. "There is more. The Marines that I was with had bonded with me and refused one scientist's orders to fire on me when I picked up something he had not recognized. He asked me what it was, and I said it was an ancient artifact from Veld. He insisted I give it to him, and I said I would only give it to an elder from Veld. He threw a fit and ordered the Marines to take it from me.

They just looked at me with a high five, and I turned to wait for the skip ship, but as I was leaving, he ordered the Marines to fire on me. They wouldn't, so I took over the small ship and 1came down here to wait until the elders on Veld could decide what should happen with the artifact. They will make arrangements to move it."

Listening to his words, made her believe that something didn't make sense. If the government of Veld knew he had something that belonged to them, then dialog would be taking place between them and representatives of the Marine Space Corp and Earth and perhaps the Corporations who had sponsored the investigation to the container out in space.

Now that she was looking at him, she felt she was getting the truth. "If you are so ferocious in your shifted form, why was a single tracker hired to retrieve you and the artifact?"

"They knew the tracker wouldn't be able to retrieve me. You were set up. Someone wanted you to fail. Someone wanted your company out of the way."

Letting out a deep sigh, she tried to answer his question. "There is no real company. There is only my father and me. We are the only ones that take on the contracts. Sometimes we work together. As I got older, we tried to take on contracts that we both could complete. There is no big company."

Zander picked up a small stick and stirred the fire, making sparks follow the smoke upward. "When you told me you were dead, you indicated that you had failed. Did you mean that you couldn't go back to your father and tell him you had failed? Have you or your father ever failed to complete a contract?"

Watching the sparks, she shook her head. "Of course, we have never failed a contract. We have turned down some, but any that we accept we complete to the limit of the details of the contract."

"Hmm," That was the sound she heard from the tall man. "Wait, what does that sound mean?"

"What was the contract that your father is supposed to be handling?"

Shit. There was a problem, and she needed to warn him. "He is on Mars. He is rescuing a Senator's daughter." Her voice was slow as she thought out the words.

Brenna brought her eyes from the sparks back to his face. She raised her eyebrows. "He is excellent in off ship suits. He has done several contracts involving worlds or moons that did not have atmospheres."

Zander put the stick into the fire and spread his hands. "So you were incidental. They wanted your father to fail."

Jumping up and pacing in her bare feet she was in her first panic in her entire life. "Oh my God, oh my God. There is no way to warn him. We remain incommunicado when out on contracts. He has no way to contact me until I return to Earth. Shit, shit, shit."

She came back to the fire. The heat felt good even on her pink toes. "So, you are supposed to kill me."

"Brenna, I am like those Marines on that container. I don't kill at the orders of some crazy scientist or without good reasons to protect others. I told you before; I am not going to hurt or kill you."

Going down on her knees, she looked directly across the fire to ask her next questions. "So now that someone is out to shut my company down and kill my father, at least tell me what you are and what was the artifact you took from that space container."

On her knees she watched him bow his head as he thought through his answer. Finally, he stood up.

"Forgive me; I must undress to show you everything."

Brenna still waited on her knees as he pulled off the heavy boots and took off his pants. She preferred not to take in the details of him as a naked male, so she kept her eyes on his head so high above her.

He took the shirt off and bent over to lay it on the pile and then reached across the fire to hand her a thin plain gold bracelet that had been around his wrist.

She turned the light bracelet in the fire that glowed in a warm reflection of red. It was smooth but in the flickering light, she could see that on the inside there were tiny words engraved in lots of loops in what looked like some ancient language.

"That is the artifact." His voice reached her from his height.

She shook her head. How could this thin gold bracelet cause such conflict?

Zander looked down at her as he drew on his beast as he spoke. "The engraving tells the story of what is happening to me."

Holding the bracelet, she looked up and was shocked to see Zander grow. He had been a big man who was at least seven feet tall, but there was a quick transformation taking place to his body. He got taller and wider. His hands grew longer with heavy thick claw-like nails on his hands and feet.

His face got a wilder, meaner look with his hair filling out around his shoulders and into furious eyes. There was a darker look to the tanned skin that stretched over large impressive muscles that seemed to be tougher than the material of her light-weight shield suit.

There was no doubt that in this form he could take on and survive any one of the reptiles on this planet. He was impressive and terrifying. Yes, her contract here was meant to end in defeat.

She took a deep breath . . . afraid to move in front of such a large threat. This large male shape was a bigger threat than the animals making noises out in the forest.

Suddenly Zander turned and took a jump that was higher that a man or most animals could make, he disappeared into the darkness, making a noise of a crash in the distant forest.

Sitting there on her knees in a frozen posture, not only her body but also her mind was inactive. Nothing was working until her legs began to complain and she had to move. She got up and found where he had stacked some additional wood for the fire. She also found her clothes and weapons.

She put a couple of logs on the fire and then put on clothes but waited to put on her shoes later. She avoided the weapons except for picking up the rifle in case another animal besides Zander wandered near this site.

Looking around for a safe place to wait for the beast to return, Brenna saw some stumps and broken trees. The trees had been down long enough for mold and some small ferns to grow on them and under some as they were held up on the stumps.

Building the fire larger she moved over and sat down to lean in against a stump. Now she felt her back was secure, and she would see anything in front by the light of the fire.

Chapter Nine

It was the smell of hot meat cooking that woke her up. Brenna hadn't meant to fall asleep in such a dangerous situation, but she was still propped up against the stump with her rifle across her lap.

She only blinked away the gray behind her eyes and saw Zander, back in a normal form and dressed, hunched over at the fire. He had some large chunk of something on a stick over the fire, supported by a couple of other sticks. It all looked very prehistoric and fit into this scene with some night bird calling out in the trees.

She got up and went to her backpack to fish out a bottle of water. "I am so screwed up in my mind. I have gone for days without sleep, and I fell asleep in this forest with a lot of animals that would like me for a snack."

He moved around the fire to face her. "Well, how about a snack on a local animal?"

This time, she took a seat beside him. He had the bracelet back on his wrist. Brenna couldn't remember what she had done with it, but he had evidently found it and put it back on his body. After what she had seen, there was no safer place for the artifact.

She handed him the rest of her water as he cut off a piece of meat and handed her the knife with the meat stabbed on the end. They both said, "Thank you," at the same time and began to eat.

She felt juice drip down her chin and decided this was much better than the pressed food bars in her backpack.

"Have you thought more about who wants you out of business?" Zander asked with his mouth around a big chunk of meat he was eating.

"It doesn't make any sense. Why wouldn't they want the Senator's daughter saved? I don't know what I will do without my father in this universe."

"I think it is the Marines," he spoke and then began to chew some more.

Brenna quit chewing and looked at him. "I thought you said the Marines were on your side?"

He nodded. "The grunts and the guys at the bottom are honest, but the ones who run the show in some faraway place sometimes have a different agenda."

The meat was good, and she knew she needed the protein, but what he was saying made her lose her appetite. What could she do if the entire Marine Space Corps was out to get her and her father?

"Is that the way it is with the government on your planet?" She looked at him wondering how much he knew about what was going on in the universe.

Brenna heard his deep sigh. "We have found we are not the norm in a government or people as compared to the rest of the inhabited worlds in our near universe.

We call those who represent us in important matters elders, but they are not always older. They are individuals who have tapped into the memories of our world. Outsiders never quite understand that process any more than they understand the change that I can control within my body.

Unfortunately, each off world that has faced us has had to accept the facts when faced with them. Some, like the men from Wisoo, get greedy and try to find what we are is a tangible thing to copy and use. Some, like the men from Earth, get greedy and smart and offer partnerships."

He stopped and sliced off another chunk of meat. He took

a bite and chewed. Brenna sat and waited for him to continue and her patience paid off.

"We are an older race than any of the peoples that we have come in contact with, as worlds have progressed with space travel. The people that have visited us we have studied. We have found you all have one thing in common. You progress and grow, but you do not control your birth amount. You all have too many children until you outgrow your world, using up its natural products and needing room for your people.

So, you all go into space. What we did eons ago, was to decide to protect the world we were on and left it intact for future generations. The answer meant birth control. It meant finding other ways to live on our planet without disturbing it. We found ways for our scientists to study the stars and the basic elements in order to build things to make our lives easier without hurting our planet.

Our people learned about our bodies and how to heal them and how to prevent diseases. Somewhere, so long ago we have no written record of it, the elders developed memories. Somewhere warriors were needed to protect the families from jungle animals and off-world invaders, and there were a few male children who could modify their bodies in time of threats."

He held up his wrist that had a thin gold bracelet circling his tan skin. "This ancient wristband tells an old story that belongs on my planet."

Looking at the meat on the end of the knife she held, Brenna suddenly realized she could eat. She bit another chunk and chewed, letting the rich juice slide down her throat. Eating gave her time to think over everything that this tall man/beast had told her. She believed him.

She had heard stories about the mysterious jungle world of U231Z42 and the fact that it was restricted. It was not one of the worlds open for tourists and definitely not one open for migration. There was a satellite with a minimal crew above the planet. That was about all she knew. No one had told her about men who turned into beasts from that planet or any other. Brenna felt this was a nightmare.

She swallowed and laid the rest of her meat down on a rock near the fire.

"I can't go back without you. I have no way off this planet, and I have no way to contact my father to warn him of the danger. I'm not sure who is after him on Mars. He can take that megalomaniac that has the child, but if your ideas are correct there has to be some trap waiting for him."

She got up to pace and immediately stepped on a sharp stone. "Shit, shit, shit." Shit was becoming her favorite word.

"Sit down and take care of your foot." Zander was at her side holding out her backpack. She looked up at him and nodded. Pacing in bare feet on a prehistoric planet was not smart.

She sat down and began pulling things out to find the small first aid pack. There was a loud clank and Zander picked up something metal that gleamed.

"What are these?"

She gave a short laugh. "Those are state of the art handcuffs made from Inconel metal. It is supposed to be unbreakable. And this," she pulled out a flat metal item that when she shook, it expanded, "is a box made of the same metal to hold the artifact."

She found and put antiseptic on her foot along with a bandage while the big man played with the handcuffs.

He looked at her with the metal in his hands. "If you caught me and got the artifact, where were you to take and deliver me?"

Looking over to where he had pulled out her backpack she saw her clothes. "I need to get dressed."

He pulled the clothes and her boots over to her so she could reach them. "Brenna, where were you told to deliver me and the artifact to, and who was going to receive me?"

She straightened out her pants and still sitting down, began to pull the tight, strong material up over her legs. "The contract was with a company called Choban, Inc. They had a special location outside of Virginia that I believe is a military location."

"Brenna, listen carefully as this is important. Tell me the exact route you would take if you captured me. Tell me every stop, each change of ship, all of the information."

She shifted on the ground to work her pants up into place and reached for socks and her boots next. "Why?"

"Because you are going to put these cuffs on me, put whatever you have in that pack that you brought to cover my head and stuff a big rock in that metal box and call the skip ship for a successful retrieval."

Now she stopped fiddling with her clothes and looked at him. "You are putting yourself in danger."

He rattled the cuffs. "I can break these in this form; I can tie them into a pretty bow for you in my modified form. I will not be in danger. But somewhere in the trip, there must be a way to warn your father or get to Mars to help him. It is our only chance."

Within the time it took her to get dressed in her dark green and black work clothes, she told him all the details she could think of—including their friend who handled equipment in Detroit where the small space ships landed. She explained that from there she was to take him on a local flight to the location in Virginia where they would meet a representative of Choban.

According to her contract, they would take possession of the box and the thief, and she would immediately receive payment.

Chapter Ten

None of the people on any of the retrievable ships were comfortable with her large prisoner. She wasn't sure that she was comfortable with the man/beast either, but she trusted him to help her save her father.

So she kept her complete uniform on, including the head and face covering, and had her rifle pointed at him all the time. He had his hands in the handcuffs that were Inconel metal that was supposed to be unbreakable.

His head was covered fully with a soft dark bag tied at his neck. He had assured her he had full use of all his senses and that no one could come up to him with a sneak attack. She noted he never stumbled as she led him from place to place and seemed to avoid items that might be a hazard.

She did think that if they could rescue her father, she might accept his invitation to visit his planet. She wanted to see what a Bensail cat looked like in its natural habitat. She wasn't sure she wanted to see this beast in his natural habitat.

When they got off the grabber ship that was floating above Earth and onto the small spaceship that would take them down to Detroit, several Marines moved out of the way to give them room to sit down. In fact, the space enforcers moved over and gave them more room than they needed. Brenna was feeling the effects of the long trip and having to be alert all of the time. They had been so far out that there had been two grabber ships with a skip ship between the two large ships. The small ship took more time to travel between and meet up with the large grabber ships than the trip the last grabber ship took to get to Earth.

During the whole trip, Zander said nothing and made no complaints. He obeyed her orders to stand and move when it was time to go from one point to another, and she wondered if he could see through the heavy material over his head or just could sense where he could place his feet.

They dropped straight down for a soft landing in what was Detroit's Spaceport. There was a short trip to the local Airport where they would take a flight to Virginia.

Ignoring the signs that told of the tunnel trains going to the airport, she led her prisoner out the front door and pushed a button to call an automatic taxi. In the cab of the taxi, she told the instruction mode to take them to the airport.

She took his head cover off and removed the handcuffs. He stretched for a moment and looked at her with a smile. "I have to find a place for men to relieve themselves."

Laughing, she nodded as she spoke. "At the airport, while you are in the men's room, see if you can find a man big enough that you can take something like his shirt or jacket. Change your looks so when you come back out, you are going to go out the closest exit to the street. I'll meet you."

The cameras saw a tall, fat man with a floppy cap and a young boy getting into an automatic taxi. It raised no flags as everyone was looking at the entrance to the flights to Virginia. The alarm went out when she and her prisoner wasn't on the second flight.

By that time she was within the large warehouse of her contact in Detroit. She used his banking system that was flipping through the strange banking network that floated through the air on Earth. Banks had become paranoid for good reasons and had developed their own complex methodology on the Matriarch where everything was stored, and it did not use electronic systems. They used memories buried in the cells of metal.

Most people, including Brenna, had no idea how it worked except it fluctuated, and one bank could not break into or communicate with another. No government agency or any hacker could find anything but tarnished bars of steel.

Brenna transferred a quarter of a million credits to the warehouse contact, and they had their pick of clothes, transportation, and information. Anything the military had was available for them. She didn't care if she used up all of their savings as it was important to have the right equipment to save her father.

Making no comment to the transaction, Zander began looking for an off ship suit in his size. At one time the suits that protected people in space were just called space suits. They were bright white and very bulky. There were large recycling air packs and strange contractions for the way the arms and knees could bend. Now the tight, lightweight suits were called off ship suits. The air recycling was a very small unit attached to the round helmet. The gloves were so precise that a coin or a small screw could be picked up between the thumb and forefinger. The tight suits allowed full movement. Brenna's contact had to help Zander make some adjustments, but there were tall men in space.

The owner seemed to be more interested in helping them when Brenna mentioned that she thought her father might be in trouble, and they were going on a secret mission to give him some help.

He brought out a couple of new weapons that would shoot better in airless conditions, but could easily be switched over to gravity or air circumstances.

Now he needed to get them onto a local space ship to Mars. That involved putting on their off ship suits and getting into a couple of sealed metal containers that he would have a local competitor that owed him credits, ship the containers to Mars. Unfortunately, it would take a couple of days, as anything faster would cause questions.

They ate lightly, hooked up their bladders to tubes in the suits and climbed into the containers.

Now all they could do was pray to their own individual Gods.

For Brenna, it was the worst two days and one night in her life. Total darkness and a lot of bumping with a point of weightless feeling left her with nausea. You could do a lot in the smooth tight fitting off ship suits, but you couldn't throw up in the helmet.

Her nameless contact had wrapped them in old-fashioned bubbled wrap so that they would not make a noise as the containers were jostled. The containers were marked HANDLE WITH CARE. She learned from personal experience that those words carried little meaning to dock handlers.

She knew from the green time on the built-in clock on the inside of her wrist that it was the end of the second day. They were told not to release the container lids until an all clear sensor lit up before their helmets.

Those last few minutes were just too long. Brenna was reaching up to push the release when the all clear light and the lid clicked open. As she sat up, pushing the wrap away, she saw Zander seated in the container next to hers; the lids had both opened at the same time.

From the way the light of her suit reflected, she realized they were in a place without an Earth norm atmosphere. Her weight and movements let her know she was on Mars. Mars had gravity, but it was less than on Earth.

She clicked on the private contact mic that would let her talk to Zander. "Looks like we got to Mars, but now we have to find the mining site and my father."

"You have some idea of this planet so that I will follow your lead."

For some reason, it pleased her that the tall man gave in to her leadership. In her mind, she had a map of the location of the unused mining operation. What they had to do was steal one of the expensive and necessary over land movers.

Her contact felt there would be a couple in this location due to all the shipping supplies moving through this area.

"Zander, we go out and try to look like we belong here. We need to find the vehicle fast." "Brenna, how do we make ourselves look like we belong here?"

"I'll show you when we find a way outside."

Fortunately, there was a red exit light over a small door that led them out into the weird night of Mars. With the thin dust that moved, the night was black with no shadows and stars above shining bright.

The first she did was to begin to throw dust up onto the shoulders of Zander's suit. He got the idea and repeated the process to show that she had been on dusty Mars for some time.

It was a useless effort as there was no one around at this time of night. In the lighter gravity, they were able to cover some distance comfortably as they walked around the warehouse buildings lined up next to each other. A lot of the living quarters were underground to avoid the dust storms and stray small rocks or asteroid hits.

The overland vehicles were strange little flat broad things and low to hang onto the ground. They had tracks that would dig into the dust and crawl over the rocks. Going through the long dust storms they would not turn over, they just dug in and continued through the gray and red plumes to come out past the disturbance.

There were two sitting between a couple of warehouses, but it was easy to see that one was out of order as the top was off and pieces of track were sticking out, partially hid by dirt. She had to wonder if they were both out of order. Maybe that was why they were sitting out here.

Zander pulled the back hatch open and crawled inside.

She worked her own way in and moved to the driver's seat. In this case, the driver's seat was in the middle up front with two seats close to it. She had driven one of these vehicles on the moon and figured she had the experience. She carefully checked out all the equipment, turning on dials, and reading screens that floated up with information. Finally, she hit the function switch, and the motor turned over smoothly.

This was more luck than she expected.

Deciding to make this look like an average run, she turned on all standard lights inside and out and pulled away from the warehouses.

"There is plenty of charge on the engine, Zander. We will be able to get to the mining area by noon. We will have to keep our suits on as these vehicles don't provide atmosphere."

"No problem."

She heard his voice in her ear bud.

It suddenly dawned on her that Zander was in a tight fitting off ship suit. When he turned into his beast form, he grew really big and would tear that suit all to pieces. She didn't think the beast could live without air on dusty Mars. Brenna didn't want to talk to him about that type of problem.

CHAPTER ELEVEN

Dawn came instantly on Mars with almost no atmosphere to break up the rising sun. What people had to get used to were all the harsh dark shadows the sun created, especially at dawn and sunset.

The sun that was a little small due to the distance still seemed too bright due to the lack of air on this red planet. For Brenna, it created a small problem as she knew she was close to the different mining sites, but black shadows hid these entrances.

It was Zander's better eyes that pointed to two places that had small buildings and stacks of composite material piled around the entrances. She drove by the first one, and it looked like it hadn't been used in years. Going to the second one that was starting to show in the sun, it could be seen that someone was going in and out on a regular basis.

Even though she was losing time, she turned around and drove to the mine that seemed to be deserted. It was in a position that would be in shadow all the time. Looking at the entrance, she decided she could drive the vehicle into the mine for some distance. The lights of the overland were bright enough to show the entire tunnel from wall to ceiling. Deep enough into the tunnel, tracks began to show in the dust of the floor. Someone had come this way recently.

"Zander, I think we need to leave the vehicle here."

Without a comment, Zander had the back hatch open and worked his big body out to wait for her. They went down the tunnel side by side with their weapons set for non-atmosphere firing capability. Ten minutes down the hall they came to a closed airlock.

She nodded for Zander to go first, ahead of her. She watched his back as he opened the lock and entered. At this point, she had to trust his stronger instincts as to rather the inside lock was safe. He waved her in, so she closed the lock behind her and began to feel and hear the air pumping into the small enclosure.

Zander opened the inside door and stepped into the tunnel. There were long life blue lights embedded in the ceiling of the tunnel. The tunnel had been made safe by a sprayed coating that kept stray rocks from falling and still allowed a view of the strata.

The floor was covered with metal and in some places wood. Brenna understood the metal plates, but she had to wonder where the miners got wood to waste on flooring. To bring wood to Mars was an expensive project and usually, it was only in furniture for the very wealthy.

The heavy boots of the off ship suits either rang on the metal or thumped on the wood. There was no quiet way to walk in these suits, but Brenna didn't want to suggest taking them off. If they got to an area of damage in these tunnels, the suits would save them. She did feel they could release their helmets. The suits have several ways of releasing the helmets. She felt that releasing them and unhooking the clamps and letting them hang down the back was the best way to keep the helmets with them without having to carry them under an arm.

Fixing hers first, she stopped Zander and soon has his hanging on his back. He had to lean down due to his tall head being above hers, but they soon were on the hunt again.

Zander stopped and lowered his rifle. "There is no way prints will show on this clean flooring."

She agreed. Either the filters on the air vents were very

good or something cleaned this floor on a regular basis. Miners wouldn't clean a floor. Miners left dirt and dust and messes, and they were dirty themselves, with no time to take a bath in these dry mines on Mars.

The water they found on Mars was either so deep below the surface that it took large equipment to pump it up, or it was tapped from the small frozen areas of the poles. Frost sails were all over to collect the water crystals that floated in the dust storms.

Water was worth a lot of credits and along with other ores, water was also what the miners were digging for in this dusty ground.

The two of them tread for miles, finding nothing pointed out that anyone had been in this mine except for the clean floors. They took a break and drank some of that precious water and ate energy bars.

"My senses say something is wrong here. But, I am not used to this planet and its energy. I can't tell what is around us except that the rocks and ground have been disturbed." Zander placed his head against the coating on one wall and closed his eyes like he was waiting.

Nervous energy gave her a need to move her feet, so she got up to start ahead and turned down a side tunnel. She glanced back at Zander's tall figure leaning against the wall as she stepped forward. With her head turned she felt the floor fall away as her body was pulled downward by Mar's gravity into darkness.

While she was still falling she saw the door above slam up and close. All light was gone as she slammed onto the hard rocks and she was unconscious as her head hit something.

The next thing she was aware of was a light in her eyes, and it hurt deep in her head. She tried to raise her hands to push the light away and felt some sting at her neck.

"Good night. Princess."

Brenna heard the voice and knew it wasn't Zander's. At least the light went out.

When she woke up, she was without her off ship suit. She had on the socks and the soft under suit that people put on to wear in comfort and to walk around waiting to get into space.

She was comfortable, but would have to stay in areas that had an atmosphere. She was now a prisoner on Mars. She was really beginning to feel like a failure again. She had to say she was not comfortable because she had a headache as she felt the side of her hair where she slammed down through the trap door.

There was a new skin bandage on the side of her head, so someone had administered medical care. Getting up, she decided she was in a bunkroom. It was cleaner than what she thought miners stayed within, so it belonged to someone else. She looked up and saw the floating camera and knew she was under someone's eyes. She tried the door anyways, but there was no hand or palm control on the inside.

Leaning against the door, she examined the room. The wall across from the door was rock with the clear seal over it. All the rest, including floor and ceiling, were metal. There were covered lights in all four corners that were on at a low setting and made the room without shadows. Either someone had built this room for permanence or she was in a holding cell.

The room had two bunks hanging on one wall, and she had woken up on the bottom one. There was a small table bolted to the floor with a canteen lying on it. In the corner, without any privacy was a standard toilet and sink, both were metal.

Again, these could be standard for a miner's room or a holding site. Of course, the missing door handle told an interesting story along with the floating camera.

She had been taught that while in the field, get rest whenever the opportunity presented itself.

She went back to the bunk and stretched out and closed her

eyes.

Sleep didn't come, as she worried about her tall beast/ man, but she did run over everything that had happened since she landed on Mars. The container she and Zander had been shipped in was made from recycled material.

Earth had a lot of junk, and everything was recycled. It included food, paper, metal and wood. Actually, wood was so rare and so important that it was used only as decorations and furniture for the very rich. Items that had been made from wood centuries ago were now made from other inventive items like moss and algae that made paper and cloth. Some time ago a smart lab rat had found a way to combine it all together, add some bonding agent that had some new stronger metal cells to it and you had a strong, lightweight material that could be poured quickly into any shape and when heat was added it became a very strong composite item.

It turned out to be exactly what was needed for shipping objects out in space where weight was important. There were sections here on Mars and on satellites that have whole walls and rooms of stacked containers with some glue.

Now, she thought about the metal walls in this room. For a couple of centuries that this planet had been bombarded with space debris from Earth and eventually with space travelers from other worlds, abandoned crafts, pieces, and junk were left behind. Everything was put to use, as the ore that was mined in this world was too expensive to smelt and process. That was until the new engines that ran without electricity or oil were developed. Being a small offshoot of the grabber engines that allowed big space ships to travel across the universe, they were adapted for use everywhere power was needed.

They were engines that found small sources of power on strings that pushed out from our sun and stars and unidentifiable sources. Free power. It changed the face of economy on

Earth.

With her eyes closed, Brenna thought about the metal walls in this room. They were neat and had tight connections and corners that meant they were new metal. She wasn't sure what that information meant, but she tucked it away.

The opening of the door brought her on alert.

CHAPTER TWELVE

The two armed Marines were polite but serious. One of them held out solid boots, and Brenna didn't hesitate to take the offer and put them on over her socks. The soft socks would not give her much protection if she had a chance of escaping.

One of the men just said that the Major needed to talk to her. The other asked if she would go calmly or did they have to put cuffs on her?

"I have no problem cooperating and don't understand why I am being treated as a prisoner. I won't give you any trouble. I would like to talk to someone in charge so I can get out of here." Brenna stood up, glad the boots fit and went out the open door.

One marine led and the other walked close behind her, as they went down a hall that was a converted tunnel on one side and metal wall with doors on the other. Brenna understood she saw the standard underground construction on Mars except in the larger caverns that had been discovered.

With all the doors shut as they went down the long tunnel, she followed the lead marine as he turned into a wider tunnel and walked past other closed doors. In this tunnel, they began to pass other Marines, some without weapons and with their hands full of folders or boxes. She felt eyes on her, as she was hustled down the tunnel and finally stopped at a door.

The lead Marine knocked once and opened it. "Sir, we have the prisoner you requested." "Escort her in." The voice was sharp and definitely from one use to giving orders.

The lead Marine moved out of the way and waved her into the room. It was about the size of her cell but was made out to be an office. There were a desk and filing cabinets, all made from the compressed material, standard military. The only unusual item was the big rolling executive fake leather chair the major had his firm military ass located.

She looked at his haircut, so short she saw the scalp reflected in the bright lights of this room. He was signing a couple of papers and then pushed them back and pulled up a floating screen that had her side blacked out.

The Marine behind her tapped her on her back, and she moved into the room in front of the desk. Glancing over her shoulder, she saw the door close, and both men take positions at the door with their weapons across their chest. Did they think she was going to attack the man behind the desk?

Turning back she could see the Major as he leaned back in his comfortable chair. While he looked at the screen, she looked at him. He was probably about her height and, since she was tall for a woman from Earth, that made him average. She decided he wasn't bad looking except for his attitude. He had the superior raise of eyebrows and lift of one side of his upper lip. On top of the whole picture, his face was too clean. It wasn't that he shaved too close, it was that he used one of the depilatories that took the hairs out below the skin.

She would bet that if he stood up, he would have a silver pistol strapped to his hip. He might be good looking, but for her taste he was just a little too much military.

His military voice began to read from the screen. "You have several aliases and a whole bunch of names on exit papers. But Earth records say you were born Brenna Gunva. I am Major Fodiman. Private, get Miss Gunva a chair."

One of the Marines moved and pushed a metal folding chair forward behind her legs. She took a moment and then sat down.

He faced her, leaning his elbows on the desk. "Where are your prisoner and the artifact? You took the thief and a box with the artifact to Earth but didn't take them to Virginia. So where are they and why are you on Mars?"

Okay, her training took effect, some training that she thought she would never need, like answering interrogations. The training said you talk, but you never answered their questions.

"Major Fodoro, you are confused."

The Major huffed. "It is Fodiman. I'm not confused. What didn't you understand?" She looked over her shoulder at one Marine with a surprised look on her face.

"Don't look at the privates, look at me. Tell me how many men did you bring with you to Mars?"

She shook her head and gave him an honest answer. "No men."

The major slammed a hand on his desk. "I have nine men down and one on life support. You must have brought along a unit of troops with you. My men are fully vetted Marines."

She turned again to the Marine behind her and smiled. "I love the Marines."

There was a beep from the floating screen. She had guessed correctly; he had her on a polygraph. So far it had told him she wasn't lying, and she knew that he was not happy with those results.

The Major took a deep breath and sat back. He was smart, and he was trying to get control of a situation that someone had thrust onto his shoulders. Brenna decided he wasn't a bad man, just had what she thought of as tunnel vision.

It fit him well down here in these tunnels. His own narrow vision let him reach a decision and then hunt for evidence to prove his decision correct. His attitude was a great tool when you were in a battle with a known enemy. It didn't help in times of peace. He was a trained warrior, not an educated investigator.

With his voice under control, he tapped a couple of buttons and nodded at her. "Let's start over. Our records show that you brought a declared thief and a recovered artifact to Earth. You did not take them to Virginia to the people who contracted for Earth Government for that recovery. Where are that Velden and the artifact?"

Looking him in the eye, as her own training had taught her, she answered. "Sir, I honestly don't know at this moment. I can tell you; they are together and safe."

"So, you have them stashed away somewhere on Earth. How did you get to Mars?" He drummed his fingers on the desktop.

Brenna didn't correct his assumption of the location of Zander and his bracelet. She did need to answer his question that was hanging out there as he watched the floating screen.

"I came like everyone else, on a direct ship from Earth to Mars. And no, you won't see me on that screen at the spaceport. I was in the dark." She thought of the blackness in the container.

The major nodded. "You had a good disguise." He was flipping a couple of pages on the screen. "You have been in the field for a couple of years and probably are very good at disguises."

He looked over to meet her eyes, and she didn't shift away. "How many men did you bring with you?"

"None." Brenna hoped that the fact that the word 'men' in the Major's mind referred to someone from Earth blood. It didn't refer to a person from another planet. His quirky decision- making within his mind would be his undoing for his military life.

"I don't like coincidences, Miss Gunva. Why the hell are you on Mars?" Tell some truth and keep the major confused. "I'm here to help my father."

"Wait." Major Fodiman was pushing transparent buttons on a ghost on his desk. "Ah, your father is Hian Gunva. You say he is on Mars?"

"Yes, we had two connected contracts. I got mine done and came to see if I could help him so we could get paid." Now was a good time to shut up.

"What is the Mars contract?"

"Sorry, under the terms of our contract, I can't share information."

Major Fodiman stood up and leaned forward with his hands on the desk, his arms supporting him. "I am an officer of the Space Marine Corps. I have clearance for top secret information."

"Okay, contact our government through Choban, Inc. Choban is who we have the off system contract with and have them give me permission through the government's information agency to release Secured details to you. Then I will answer your questions. While we wait, I'm going to need some decent food. I can eat with your own men, so one of these Marines can show me to the cafeteria."

The major sat back down, as her words took the air out of his balloon. He wasn't about to contact Choban, and he didn't want those above him to think he had a situation he couldn't handle.

For Brenna, she had learned that Zander was in the area and out of his off ship suit. From the sound of the destruction, Zander was also in his shifted mode.

"Gentlemen, escort this individual back to her holding room." He was still leaning forward and frowning at her.

"And my meal, sir?"

Now he slumped back down in his expensive chair. "Get her a meal in her room, and get her a uniform or something to wear."

Brenna smiled as she led the two Marines out of the room.

She licked her fingers and walked near the covered rock wall of the tunnel. She ran her wet fingers along the covering hoping it would leave a trace of her scent. Brenna had already learned that Zander had a high sense of smell. She hoped she was leaving her personal odor along this wall.

She was almost back to her room, wetting her fingers two or three times before one of the men objected. She decided not to argue with them, as she was hoping for allies. She did take a second and kiss the outside of the door as she went inside.

"Home sweet home." She winked at the men as she stepped back from the quick kiss and went in to sit on the lower bunk. The Marines didn't enter but closed the door as soon possible.

Grateful for the boots, she took them off and sat them under the bed and stretched out to be comfortable. Closing her eyes, she thought about what she had learned and what was still missing about her mission. For one thing, she still didn't know where her father was and if he might be in these tunnels or in connected mine shafts.

With the sound of the door opening, she sat up to see the two Marines entering. One had a tray that had to be food, and the other had a stack of clothing. They sat their loads down on the small table, looked at her and left. The click of the lock as the door shut told her she was definitely a prisoner.

The fact that they returned with the food and clothing told her that everything was close.

They were not spread out in the tunnels but were in a small, maintained section.

Years of training to observe made her notice the two Marines were letting down their guard with her. They didn't keep a grip on their weapons; in fact, they had no control over the weapons while they carried items. When they sat their items down, they turned their backs on her and left the room. They didn't feel threatened by her.

Chapter Thirteen

Brenna had lots of time to think within the confines of the metal room within the tunnels of Mars. Near the two sites of groups of settlements that might be stretched to be called cities, a large amount of the living space was underground.

It was more efficient for air production, air cleaning, and air storage to contain it within shafts that could be sealed with the cheap clear coating.

The tunnels would travel for hundreds of miles in all directions and seldom ran into barriers that could stop the burrowing. There were many levels going down, one tunnel below another. There were extensive tunnels with complete apartments and storage for anything, no matter how bulky.

Initially, the tunnels were just mining shafts that had been closed up with air locks with connecting composite shacks above ground. The dust storms made moving around on the surface problematic, so the mineshafts began to be connected.

With immigration and technology, over a couple of hundred years, Mars had a lot of residents and a couple of spaceports. The mining had almost become obsolete, but no matter where the mines had been located, they were usable and worth some value.

What had come next for the abuse of Mars, was the deep well drilling. The drilling was going after pockets of gas of various types, water, and a type of extraction drilling that pulled metal and gemstones from a single hole.

Earth had been mismanaged through such overuse and overpopulation that its people began to spread out into the universe to find new homes. The people of Earth did the same mistreatment of Mars.

Brenna was thinking about all of this as she was wondering exactly which tunnel her father might be located in, as he hunted for the senator's daughter.

He was walking into a deadly trap if he hadn't already fallen down one like she did in her Marine trap. She washed up at the small sink, used the toilet knowing that the camera was in the room and put on the loose older military clothes. They didn't fit well, but they were clean and had all the closures still intact.

Everything she needed to find her father had been removed efficiently when she was unconscious, so she needed Zander to find her. She could only hope that he could take her to wherever he had deposited his items before he changed into the beast to protect himself from the Marines.

Lying on her back, she was looking up at the metal ceiling past the upper bunk. Why did they have a metal ceiling instead of the tunnel rock with a clear coating like the one side of this room? Because there was something above her room, silly girl, she answered herself.

Okay, she could climb up on the upper bunk and push against some of the metal to see if she could get any of the pieces lose. She looked over at the floating camera and wondered how long it would take a couple of Marines to come through that door to pull her off the top bunk?

She made it through the rest of the day with another meal delivered by one Marine while the other leaned against the wall outside. This time, they waited with the door open while she ate. They talked quietly to each other but looked over at her. The looks were not threatening, more of interest.

After the tray was removed and the door was locked with the regular click, she decided to do some exercises. She didn't want to do anything to prove her strength, so she just did some yoga. Using water at the sink, Brenna cleaned out her mouth and then lay down on the lower bunk. She wasn't down very long before the lights went out, leaving her in the dark except for the red light on the camera.

She didn't feel sleepy, so she spent some time thinking again about the maze of tunnels on Mars. She froze when she heard a slight rustle about where the camera was located. She didn't want to look in that direction as she was sure the camera had night vision as well as heat scan.

Out of the corner of her eye, she saw the red light go out. What the hell was going on? Those were her first thoughts. Her next one was to move and to move fast. She didn't need lights to reach up to the top bunk. Holding onto the edge of the bed above, she pulled herself up and over to kneel on the thin mattress above.

Next, she did something that most would call stupid. She held her arms out over the edge of the bunk and leaned until she almost fell forward. Suddenly two large rough hands with long claws wrapped around her wrists and pulled her away from her place and upward. Brenna knew she was being pulled through the metal ceiling, so she trusted the hands that held her.

She might be blind in this darkness, but the owner of those big clawed hands could see without light. Praising the fates that she had kept boots and all on when she laid down on the bunk, she was on her back on the metal that she thought was the ceiling of her room.

Unusually large muscular arms wrapped around her, pulling her up tight against a warm body. Without hesitation, she had her legs up around a waist that was like a tree trunk and her arms were above broad shoulders around a neck that was as thick as a Marine's leg.

There was a second of hesitation as he got a whiff of her hair and he took that second to push his nose down by her ear. Then with a snort, he was moving.

Brenna hung on until she began to tire, as they crawled through the space between the two floors of metal cabins. She assumed that the one she had been in was the lowest and that there could be several floors above it and space between for utilities.

"Zander, I hope you are getting close to where you stashed your closes. I have never traveled this far upside down. I lost all my things as I fell into a trap. I need your equipment to contact my father. I don't think we are in the right tunnel." She whispered knowing he would hear her words.

She felt him take one long arm and swing it under her to pull her to him and help relieve some of the stress on her limbs. He moved forward again in the blackness like a three-legged hound dog. It didn't seem to slow him down.

There was a glimpse of light over the beast's back, as a piece of metal on the seam above didn't fit smoothly. As they moved forward there began to be more loose seams and even below them, a light gleamed upward.

They must be coming into an area that was not inhabited and with no maintenance. Brenna thought that Zander must have found a good place to hide his clothes and shift into something that could take out armed Marines.

Their trip must be over, as her ride stopped and the beast bent down to lower her back to the metal. He removed his arm from her waist, and she unhooked her legs. Brenna was able to see with enough with light showing through the metal from below. Now she could see that the area above was rock covered in the usual transparent coating.

Zander put a large clawed hand on her chest when she started to move. "Okay, big guy. I get the message. I will just lie here waiting for large Martian spiders to crawl over me and try little bites to see if I taste good. Do you see any bugs over there?" He was gone.

How could something so large move so fast and so quietly? Brenna slowly rolled over to see a whole panel missing. Pulling herself to the edge, she dropped her head and shoulders over to look around.

She had a great view of Zander in his regular male form and a fine naked ass. He was stepping into pants and pulling them up over his legs. Catching the edge, she did a flip and dropped down to the floor of the tunnel below.

This tunnel was full of broken and discarded supplies. There was a small amount of red dust on most of the containers and broken items, so Brenna decided they had been here for a while.

"Zander, you found a nice hideaway. But there are miles and miles of tunnels, and I need to find my father. If someone is trying to kill him or set him up for a mishap, I need to get to him."

"I know, but I am not familiar with this planet. The smells in these tunnels are so mixed and some so old I smell acid. I can back you up, but I don't think I can go ahead of you to lead you to your father."

Brenna felt her clothes were adequate, so as long as they stayed inside of tunnels with airlocks, they would be okay. On the other hand, her father might be in a mining shaft that was not connected to this unit.

"Zander, I don't know if your sense of direction has kicked in yet, but we need to go in the direction where the sun rises on this planet. We will call that east, and we might even have to travel away from it at times to find connecting tunnels or avoid Marines."

"I understand and can lead the way to protect you."

Zander had his weapons, but he did hand her a long knife. As she walked behind him, she picked up a long piece of metal pipe. It was rare to find metal just lying around not being put to use in some manner on Mars.

Watching his smooth, quiet movements, she decided he was as good-looking all over as his handsome face. Then she shook her head and knocked all thoughts of interest in the Veldan who was helping her to find her father. She was a tracker and like her father would grow old alone.

Thinking of her father, it dawned on her that he once had someone in his life. Her father had to have spent some time with her mother. Why had she never asked about her mother? Again she shook her head as she needed all her attention on the trek through the tunnels.

Chapter Fourteen

During their long trip through the strange conglomerate of passages under the crust of Mars, Zander was the one who decided when and where they would sleep. He was the one who told her to hide while he would disappear and come back with food and water.

Zander was the one who kept up the pace through the mixture of tunnels always seeking an eastern passageway. There were times when they had to travel at night though inhabited sections to avoid civilians.

Once, in the middle of sleep, he woke her and handed her a pulse rifle. Can you hug a guy who brings a weapon and not flowers? Geez. Even her dad would approve of this gift. To top it off it was on full charge.

No, shake it off, Brenna. They weren't on a date; they were on a hunt to save her father.

Besides, trackers didn't date.

It was on the fourth night, as she tried a special tap on Zander's ear bud that she got a return signal. They had kept the signals simple, just two taps then one then a long wait and repeat. "Oh, hot damn. Zander, I reached Hian. We must be fairly close."

"You're sure it is your father?"

"Yes. We have a code. He repeated it back to me. If we get closer to him, we should be able to talk to him. Let's move out."

"Wait Brenna. You need to rest. We will leave after six hours sleep."

Brenna frowned at him as she began to pick up her stuff. Somewhere along the way he had given her a solid military backpack and she kept most of her extra food and water in it along with other small things. Glancing over at Zander, she was surprised that he was stretched out on the floor with his hands behind his head.

"Get up, Zander. We need to get closer so I can talk to my father." "In six hours."

She stood and slammed her backpack down. "Zander, this is my father and my partner. You are the one who pointed out that both Hian and I were sent into traps."

"Yes, and we need to be prepared. We need to be rested and make sure we know what we are walking into so that we can really help Hian Gunva." With that, he closed his eyes.

Looking at the long body stretched out, Brenna realized the subject was closed. She wasn't about to go off on her own as he was her secret weapon.

With a deep sigh, she stretched out on the floor next to him making sure she was a couple of feet away and put her head on her backpack. Brenna felt she wouldn't sleep, but maybe she could rest her body and think about what she could do when they got up close to the danger zone. Feeling warm even on the cold floor, she was surprised that she had drifted off to sleep.

Surprised that she had gone asleep, she was aware why she was warm. She was wrapped about Zander.

"You have been asleep a little over six hours."

It was Zander's voice talking above her head. Now she was fully awake and aware that she had a leg over his body and an arm across his chest with her head on his arm. Brenna pushed away without saying anything. For the first time in her life, she felt a hot flush wash over her face and chest.

She jumped up and grabbed a water flask from her pack and emptied it over her head. The water wasn't that cold, but the air in the tunnel was blowing from some distant AC. She wished she had thought out that action for a moment or two and drank the water instead.

Digging into the backpack, she found another shirt and turning her back to Zander, Brenna changed out of the wet military top and just left it on the ground. The new one was a dark blue that Zander had found in one of his trips. He seemed to find the right size.

When she turned, he was holding out a protein bar.

"I can eat this on the way. We continue east. I'll keep your earbud and every hour I will try to reach Hian."

They only walked for ten minutes before they ran into the end of the eastern tunnel. There was no choice as the tunnel turned one direction, to their left.

It was a long tunnel that wasn't straight, with smooth turns and some tunnels that came from the direction they had come, but none going east.

"Zander, we have to stop. We are actually going further away from my father's signal. We have to find a solution."

Zander looked at the covered red rock wall that faced east. "What do you suggest, explosives?"

"No, damn. Maybe we could ask someone."

"Yes, I'm sure I could get an answer from a Marine as to how to find a way east. On the other hand, you are a pretty female. I am sure a miner would love to show you his favorite eastern tunnel."

Taking a moment to let his words sink in, she knew she didn't want him beating answers out of a Marine. It hit her that he had said she was pretty, wow.

"Okay, I vote that we go back west until we find some people and then we can react as to who the people might be. If they are Marines, you can try to talk to them and if they are civilians, I will talk."

With that decision, Brenna led the way on the next tunnel

that went back west. She hated each step that took her away from the direction that she needed to go to reach Hian.

Within an hour and after a couple of turns still going west, they heard people ahead that turned out to be civilians. She stopped and pulled out a soft sleeveless shirt and tore it up to make a head and face covering. Next, she lay down and rolled in as much dust as she could find, got a dusty red look to her clothes.

She gave her weapon to Zander but put her knife in her belt where it would be obvious. "Wait here unless I look like I am in trouble."

She came out of the side hole they had stepped into and slowly walked forward until she saw several men arguing over a piece of machinery. In some ways, her dirty clothes looked like what they were wearing, including one had rags tied over his head and face.

One of the cursing men saw her and nudged the man next to him. They looked at her with interest, but they didn't give off vibes of threats.

Looking back as if she was frightened, Brenna tried a stutter and an accent. "I, ah, need' get east. Real fast." She looked over her shoulder again.

One guy who looked harmless, glanced down the tunnel behind her to see if someone was following her. "Well, sweet thing. If you don't mind getting dirty, there is a drop down a shaft that will let you go under the barrier and join up with the big tunnels that go east."

"Thank ya'. If'n a real big guy comes this way, donna' say yo' saw me. Please."

Another guy stepped forward and pulled down his face wrap to show a lopsided smile. "I could show her."

"Ned, it is only around the second corner of the unfinished tunnel."

The smiling guy winked. "Well, if she turns the wrong way

she would be lost in these tunnels for hours. Come on green eyes; I won't let you get lost."

"Er, I donna' think that's a good idea. I can find me a way." The smile left his face as he had a hand on her arm.

"Hey, let go o' me."

There was the sound of heavy boots thumping behind them and a loud voice called out to her. "Hey gal, you trying to run away again?"

Brenna felt the man beside her let her go, and they all turned to see a tall, broad figure running toward them. He was covered in dirt and had a rag wrapped around his head. He also had a lot of weapons all over his body, inside and out of the dirty clothes he was wearing. "Fuck, look at the size of that guy."

"Is that your fucking boyfriend?"

"Hey, I ain't getting into a damn family argument."

The men were speaking at the same time as they all started backing up, putting the piece of equipment between them and the big man who shed dust as he pounded down the tunnel.

Brenna looked at the men and then at Zander and smiled, but decided to play out the scene. "Hey, honey. I sorta' got lost. Where did ya' go?"

"Shut up Bensail, and move on down the way." Zander's voice was low and sharp.

Brenna knew when a getaway was required, so she turned and ran in the direction the men had indicated had an escape tunnel to go east. With Zander on her heels and the men hiding with mouths open behind their broken machine.

Turning into the second corner, she found herself in an unfinished tunnel. Within a few feet, there was a drilled hole going down to a tunnel below.

"Zander, I need a light."

When he placed a hand flash into her hand, she turned it on and drew her arms in tight and dropped through the hole.

Fortunately, as she expected, it was a short drop as this tunnel was only about as tall as she was, not quite six feet. She smiled, thinking that her tall companion would have to stoop as they hurried through this unfinished hole through the Martian rocks.

They had worked their way through the tunnel, grateful to feel the air moving past their bodies. Brenna waved the light around, but there was only one way to go so she just moved forward knowing Zander was close.

"Honey is a sweet item made on Earth by bugs."

She stopped to hear Zander speaking behind her. The words soaked in, and he must be referring to when she had called him "honey" in front of the men. Okay, he was trying to figure out the correlation of the word.

"Zander, yes it is sweet, and it is harvested. But we also use it as a term of love or . . ." she wanted to add more because she was talking herself into a corner. "We use it as friendship, like when we talk to children and family and also lovers and . . ." shit, she really needed to shut her mouth.

"Oh. Like when I called you Bensail. It really was a secret compliment." "Hmm." She wasn't going to add anything else.

The light exposed some containers and equipment, and she decided to stop. There was also light up ahead, coming from above.

Passing her in his stooped over position, Zander began to move up on the debris. Brenna turned off the light and moved closer to watch the tall Veldan stick his head up into the next level. He disappeared, and she began to climb up containers and equipment.

She looked up to see that Zander must be lying on his stomach above, holding his arms down to reach for her. She let him pick her up and with his strength he was able to stand before he sat her down on her feet.

They were in a finished tunnel with transparent coating

and low lights set in the ceiling. The floor was metal. Right behind where they had entered was a metal wall that did not surprise Brenna. It was the end or maybe the beginning of the tunnel heading east.

Chapter Fifteen

Brenna got one nice loud repeat from her father since entering the finished eastern tunnel and then it quit. She had tried several times with no results, they just slowly moved forward into a very strange area.

They were in working mines. There were the large modern boring machines that pulled the dirt out and spread the supports were needed to keep the tunnels safe. There was no clear coating on any of the walls in these tunnels. Although there weren't any workers present, it was evident that there was new mining taking place.

"I wonder what they are mining for in this area of Mars." Brenna kicked some rocks as she mulled over her question.

"Coal." Zander held up some black rocks. "No one uses coal anymore."

"You can get oil and other products from coal. Compress it and you can get gemstones."

They moved on in the rough tunnels until Zander waved them to a stop. He waved her silently to wait as he crept forward. Brenna was always amazed that such a large person could move without a sound. Unlike her, he never stepped on a rock that made a noise or even stirred up dust. He went about ten yards and seemed to be taking deep breaths. He slowly walked backward until he turned to face her.

His voice was a whisper. "Traps. Set by one human. We need to go around, because if we disarm or trip the snares the one who set them will know someone is here."

"That is why my father has quit answering. He has tripped

one of those traps trying to disarm it. Damn. We have to find this maniac and shut him down."

"Your father might have accidently triggered a trap like you fell down the levered floor the Marines had established."

Brenna shook her head. "My father was trained by some strange people before he started teaching me. He was trained by men that had what was definitely illegal means at their disposal and worked for a government that played dirty. They eventually were dispersed, and some that were caught were either put in jail or sent off Earth. The government was overturned, and none of the officials were allowed to be part of the newly formed General Earth Government."

This whole conversation was in whispers and so close to each other that Brenna smelled the strange odor of the jungle from Zander. The sweat that stuck to his clothes just gave off the unusual fragrance of damp tropical plants. She had to shake her head again to get her mind on her father and not a tall Veldan.

Stepping away from Zander she looked around in the cave. There had been several crossing mine tunnels that they had ignored as they were intent on heading east. Looking back, she saw the most recent boring machine that they had passed.

"Hey, big guy. I wonder what the person who set those alarm traps would think if a couple of boring machines got out of control and ran into his snares?"

During the next few hours, they searched for deserted boring machines and traps. The machines were easy to find, and Brenna had no trouble moving them into place and setting up timers on the starters. What was needed was Zander's ability to sense or smell the traps.

He found several, but there were four that could be destroyed with boring machines. Doing her job, she put the machines into position, trying to be as quiet as possible with ten thousand pound rolling contraptions.

Zander had the idea to have them destroy the snares within five minutes of each other. His idea was to go in at the point of the oldest not the newest, so they would wait twenty minutes for the last machine to act.

They did wrap their faces in the rags, figuring there would be plenty of dust from some of the traps. They were wrong in one thing. There were no explosions and no dust. There was some damage to the boring machine that had gone in first. The one they intended to follow.

It had gone through a section that Zander determined was a trap and had long wires hanging off of it. It was clear that the machine had received a colossal jolt of electricity, enough to fry out the motor and to kill any human that had been driving the appliance.

The momentum of the apparatus continued far enough to drag out the wires from whatever they were attached to, so the power connection was gone. Other than a couple of sparks from one wire, the rest were dead.

It looked like an invisible electrical net that was stretched across the tunnel. It would kill the invader and notify the person who had set up the trap.

But if their theory worked out, the person who had set the trap should be busy with four alarms going off in four different locations. He might think that a unit of Marines was now coming after the senator's daughter or that something had gone wrong with his system. Either way, he would be drawn out.

Zander now had the next idea, and it was to cut off the power in this entire section of tunnels. He could feel the flow of power in the buried floor that led to the source of the central power station. Electricity was a commonly used power source on Mars since it was not practical to build large structures on the surface. The ground and rocks were ideal for the tunnels and perfected to lay down the connecting power wires that were never used on most planets.

Zander knew they couldn't get to a real center, but he felt they could take out enough local power stations to make things difficult for the man who was hiding in this location. Brenna told him that the man would have backup lighting and probably night-vision goggles. Fortunately, Zander was born with night vision.

He wasn't worried about himself when the power was taken out, but he was considering the Earth female that he had grown attached to, as they traveled together. He thought about how much trouble he was going to be in and how he would answer with the elders, as he explained why he was a thief and now had deep feelings for an alien female.

He shuddered, as he allowed his beast to settle down to wait for release. He knew what his next plans were going to require that strength. He just had to work out a way to keep the female safe.

Chapter Sixteen

Brenna had no choice but to follow Zander. He was a walking scanner of an advanced style, far beyond any that was produced for the military. She understood why Earth had been eager to sign a treaty with Veld.

The fact that one of these special warriors could be borrowed to accompany the Space Marine Corps whenever they were going into a really treacherous situation was amazing. One Veldan warrior could save the lives of the entire unit of Marines, or knock a unit of Marines out of the way. Wasn't that what she had seen when he had rescued her?

Still, to the best of her knowledge, he hadn't killed any of the Marines. He had probably broken some bones. Now she was following the walking scanner because he said he was following buried power lines to a source of energy. He had boots on as heavy as hers and was also wrapped in all the dirty rags. She also believed him. She was grateful that she had picked up a cracked pair of goggles as she rifled through debris, as they walked through the newly made tunnels. If he were going to turn the lights out, she would need to see the green things through the glasses.

Zander held up a closed fist, and she froze. He seemed to disappear instantly around a corner, but she had learned her lessons, so she stayed without making a sound. At last, his hand could be seen, waving her forward.

Stepping carefully, Brenna was surprised to find a small cavern. Unlike caverns on Earth, this was left over when Mars had water that moved and washed away soft rock. In caverns on Earth, there was hard rock with stalactites and long years of dripping water.

This cavern was a large ragged room with some smooth areas and some large rocks exposed. There was also power equipment, easy to recognize. There were a couple of tunnels leading out beside the one they entered from, and Zander was examining each without entering the openings.

The lights began to dim without going out, just a nice soft light in the cavern and down each tunnel.

"What's happening?" Zander asked over his shoulder, as he approached one of the big power units. It was a large ugly central power source with a small grabber motor buried inside and many large cables attached by bulky insulating bolts to the main frame.

Looking around, Brenna sat down her equipment, weapons, and backpack. "I would guess that the miners had this set up on Earth time. Every 12 hours it would shut down for a simulated nighttime. The miners would quit work and relax, maybe clean up and eventually sleep for six or eight hours."

The tall Veldan came over and began to stack his stuff beside hers. "Rest is a good idea. We are about six hours away from where the strange male from Earth is holding a child. Hopefully, he has your father there also, and we can save both at the same time. But it would be best to eat and drink and then get some sleep."

"I can't sleep worrying about my father. We need to continue." She moved toward a tunnel. "Careful, there are traps at the entrance of each of those."

Stopping she looked back to see him sitting down and pulling out bottles of water. She knew she couldn't go on without him, so maybe they could take a short break. She would work on changing his mind after they ate and rested.

Brenna had to admit that Zander had been right. It felt good to get water and food into her stomach and let her body stretch out on the rags on the floor. The dim light left the high cavern in darkness, so there was a feeling of closeness with her partner.

She was so aware that he was stretched out beside her and that unusual smell of jungle touched her nose. She thought about animals having sex under big leaves as soft rain pattered above. Shrugging a shoulder against the rags, she wondered if pheromones were in the sweat of the Veldan.

"Zander, what do your people think about sex?" God, had she actually asked that question.

She was relieved that he didn't jerk or jump up to move away.

There was a long pause before his deep voice answered. "We think it is enjoyable."

Now she wished she had bitten her tongue and brought up some other subject in this dim light. She thought of his eyes with the strange mixture of blue and green. They were not blue- green. His eyes had streaks of blue along with distinct streaks of dark green. It was fascinating to look at those eyes. She thought that when she was close to him, the colors moved. She had to wonder what happened to those eyes when he changed into the beast.

She felt a surge of heat in her lower body. Damn, she had been alone for too long. Then he spoke and made it worse.

"Brenna, what do your people think about sex?"

"Well, ah. I guess I could say the same thing you did. We think it is enjoyable. But we seem to kinda' mix it up with some type of traditions, emotions, and promises we don't mean to keep. It gets really complicated."

She turned on her side to face him, her head up on an elbow and cupped in a hand. She would have been okay if he hadn't turned those eyes toward her. She bit her lower lip and then did the most amazing act. She leaned forward to place her mouth against his.

There was an instant, with her eyes closed that she had time to wonder if Veldans kissed? But that was answered as he wrapped his arms around her as he began to open his lips and used his tongue to stroke her lips. She allowed him entrance and wondered how he knew what she wanted. He had always seemed to be so composed and distant until this kiss.

This kiss lets her know he was not composed, and he wasn't distant. He was into her mouth to taste it completely, and he was leaving his own taste behind. It was a taste that was different from any man that she had ever kissed going back to her first, one when she was only ten and behind the bush in what was known as Old Russia.

He spoke with his mouth against her ear, "You know with my unusual talents; I can smell you.

I know you are sexually aroused."

Lifting her head she looked at his face and now saw that his eyes had indeed changed. They were almost the dark green with almost no blue showing.

"Zander, your eyes."

"Yes, it is part of a reaction from my body in being aroused to you. But I won't continue if you say I should stop."

How could she tell him to stop with his eyes so dark green and his lips on her neck? She pushed his layers of clothes aside on his wide chest to find his hot smooth skin.

It was the only invitation he needed, and he began to work her clothes off with soft caresses. Unlike Zander, Brenna was anxious to proceed as she tugged and pushed to get his garments out of the way. She wasn't sure it would be necessary to be completely naked as her experience had been several sexual encounters with just enough pushed aside to complete the act.

Zander had another quest and it was to get his female without anything between his body and hers. Even his beast purred in agreement, as he worked to move away cloth and expose Brenna's form.

Not sure how it happened, Brenna was pleased to feel the long body of the Veldan stretched out, as he pulled her over onto him making a warm mattress of skin and muscle. He used his legs to spread hers and one long arm to reach down between them.

Immediately, he found that one spot that some amazing designer of the female form had put there only for pleasure. The small nub had no other purpose, and many had wondered why it appeared just before puberty. But Zander knew what it was for, as his long middle finger encircled it to bring her instantly to orgasm.

Brenna's nipples hardened as her lower stomach tightened. She clenched her thighs around his legs and threw her head back as she rode out the pleasure his one finger brought to her body. At last, she sank into his chest, breathing hard and wondering why it had never felt that good when that nub had been touched before.

Catching that breath, she was rolled over and looking up in the dim light as the big shadow leaned down to lick his way down to her breasts. He paid attention to each one as she locked her fingers into his hair.

"Please, Zander. I need you to fuck me."

Her answer was a deep growl as he moved up, on one hand, to use the other first to spread her wet lips below and then center his excited member to enter slowly. He might be a big male in all ways, but he was a gentle lover. He let her body adjust to his size as he pushed in steady but leisurely. Each in and out movement brought more moisture and response from Brenna.

She had her hands gripping his shoulders, not aware that her short nails were digging into his thick skin. Brenna needed that grip to let her know she was still aware of what was happening to her body. She felt another climax building and her mind was not thinking of anything but the smell of sex, the feel of sex and the release of sex.

He reached the depth he was looking for, and she had that second climax. It was her first time to have two orgasms in one act. But there was more as he pumped out and back in with soft movements that she felt from the top of her head to her toes. It must have been her blood flowing fast through her body, all of her veins and vessels contracting as her body tightened around him.

She heard the deep growls from his inner body as he bore inward again time after time and then there was a final thrust as his body went forward and he pressed against her mound and that swollen nub one more time. As his scalding semen pumped into her, she almost screamed when one more release tore through her.

Zander placed his mouth over hers to swallow the noise and prevent anyone in one of the tunnels from hearing them. He then rolled over again, pulling her on top to let them both rest. For her, she was too weak to do anything but lay her head on his chest with her eyes closed and a smile on her face.

They made love two more times that night, using different positions and tasting every part of each other's bodies. It was somewhere after relaxing after that second unusual session that she realized it wasn't sex they were doing, they were making love. How had this happened? How could she fall in love with an alien male who could turn into a frightening beast?

They finally exhausted themselves in a pleasant way and slept tangled together. The lights brightened slowly, and Brenna got up to find the old rags to wipe her body of all the moisture left from the night.

"Zander, we need to talk."

He ran a hand down her back to grip her bottom cheek. "I think we did a lot of nice things that do not need to be explained."

"You know there is no future for us."

At those words from her, he shifted his blue, green eyes to look at her. "You think we will not win the battle ahead for us?"

Shaking her head she frowned. "I always go into a battle optimistic. I mean there is no future for you and me, Zander and Brenna. This was a glorious night, but it is now morning and the night is over.

I am an Earth tracker, and you are a Veldan warrior. Our paths have crossed this one time in some way that fate decided. Last night I willingly gave you my body and somewhere during the night I gave you my heart. But when we are done with this mess, and I finally return to Earth, and you return to Veld, my heart will no longer be in my body. I will have this body, and you will take my heart. We will find a way to exist."

Zander knelt beside her, looking at her, and she did see emotions. "Why can't we be together?"

"Zander, you are not a fool. What are we going to do together? Are you going to come to Earth with me and live in a cold climate? I can see your beast going out to catch wolves when I go off on a tracking contract. Or maybe you want me to come to your jungle. I can track the Bensail for fun when a Marine unit wants to use you for a few months.

No Zander, we are two interesting beings from two alien races that are not meant to be together. I bless the fates that let me know you and let us have this one night that I will cherish forever. But once we save my father and that little girl, our relationship is our past."

He stood and looked around this unusual dusty red cave. "There has to be a way, and I will never give up looking for it because I will see your green eyes every time I lay my head down and talk to my beast."

CHAPTER SEVENTEEN

Brenna got her clothes on, layer after layer and was stooping over to tie her boots when she noticed his clothes were still piled up neatly on the floor.

She stood up and looked at him. He indeed was still in a glorious naked form. "Are you going to change into the beast to protect us?"

He nodded at something behind her and she turned to see a large catch net against a wall hidden behind one of the large generators. "Why would the maniac put a catch net back there? Is he trying to hide something?"

"I put the net up there." With those words, he turned and quickly picked her up and threw her into the air to be caught in the middle of the net. Only this Veldan beast/man had the strength to toss a tall Earth woman several feet into the air to let her be caught by a sticky net.

Brenna had used these nets to capture a lot of men and even some animals. As soon as she hit it, not only did her body stick to it, but the force of her movement caused sections to wrap around her, pinning and immobilizing her in the air. She resisted the impulse to fight the tangle, knowing it would just allow the threads of the net to swaddle her. She had seen animals get strangled, as they fought too hard and too long.

"What the hell are you doing?"

"You are right, Brenna. I too lost my heart last night. I am going to change, and I will lead your father back here to release you."

With those words, she hung in the air in anger as she

watched in the dark while he changed into what Earth scientists said was impossible. He shifted into a larger form of a miraculous beast that could control the elements around him. It had made his ancestors survive the arrows, and it made him able to survive phasers.

She started cussing and continued until her throat was sore and the beast was out of sight. Behind the large piece of machinery, she could not see which tunnel he went down or how he disarmed the traps.

It took her at least an hour of miniscule movements to get one arm free. First were the fingers, then slowly a hand, and this allowed her to slide the arm out of her jacket that was held by the sticky strands. With a full arm free, she could reach one of her many sharp toys.

Her first effort was to cut the sticky strands that had her head trapped. It was a tricky operation because as she cut the strands, if too much pressure was put on a strand, more would move in that direction. She had to slip the sharp knife behind the net and put the same push with her head as she did with the knife as she cut strand after strand.

With all of this, she had to keep her breathing slow and even so that there were no more strands moving into her body. At last, she cut a final piece that left her head free with the back of her head covered with goo. Yuck.

Now she had to get out of her top layer of clothes like an acrobat doing an act in the air. Fortunately, she could hang onto the outer clothes that were caught by the net. She kept her pants on and bent over with a groan to untie her boots and get her feet out of what she would need later. Damn.

She grunted as she hung onto her trapped jacket to pull her legs from the trousers. Now she had to push enough to fall away from the net. Hanging onto her jacket, she brought her knees up and placed her feet against the cloth. This was going to be like jumping sideways off a trampoline.

Brenna did a push, everything behind her gave away, and she did a tuck and roll. She hit the floor without much damage. Taking a moment to check herself out Brenna got up. She couldn't see much, but felt around for her backpack and her weapons. It was a short search in her bare feet to find all of her things alongside of his, behind a pile of containers.

She got a mismatched outer layer of clothes on and tried his boots, but discarded them. Their big size would be a hindrance and would not help. She took some rags and wrapped a piece of broken container material to the bottom of each foot.

She stood and stamped her feet to make sure the new shoes would work. Gathering up weapons, she looked at the implant on her wrist. Zander, in his beast mode, was almost three hours ahead of her. Not only that, in the modified mode he was fast. It would be hard to tell how far ahead in the tunnels he was before she could catch up with him.

Standing here wasn't going to help, Brenna hefted her weapon and began to search each tunnel opening to see if she could find a trace of which one he used. She only had the low light from her wrist, but she held her arm up to shine on the floor and walls.

The first tunnel had substantial damage to it, and when she threw a rock into it, the trap was down. The next looked like it hadn't been touched. Brenna just went back to the first and started tracking. If Zander had gone down this tunnel, he would have taken care of any traps.

Walking near the side of the round tunnel that still had some light, she saw no prints. At last, there were some scuff marks in the middle and damage to the round ceiling. Zander must have taken out another trap.

After another couple of hours, she took a break, relieved her bladder and filled up on water and a protein bar. Her feet were feeling the strain of walking in the wrappings, so she adjusted everything and hoped for the best.

According to her wrist, almost seven hours had gone by since Zander left her suspended on the net. Brenna had a hunch that she was going to get to the maniac's site only to find death. She had a few hours before the false nighttime and the dim lights. Evidently, a different electrical power unit supported this area, and that explained the lights.

The dusty floor was covered with footprints and drag marks. She was sure that Zander, in whatever form he took, would not leave tracks. She had followed him on a prehistoric planet and only saw prints that he wanted her to see, to lead her into his trap. These marks were possible to lead someone else into a trap.

She couldn't rest any longer, and when the lights dimmed for a night, she couldn't stop.

Watching in all directions, she saw the anomaly. There was a hole in the ceiling.

Stopping, she took the time to search quietly through her backpack for a scanner. She let it read in all directions, including above, but other than a small rodent, there were no warm bodies showing up within fifty feet of her location. The area above her was hollow. She had to wonder why a second tunnel was bored through above this one. Or was it the other way around? Had this tunnel been dug out below the one above?

Brenna knew that Zander could jump that high, but she had to find some help to get up to that upper tunnel. She scratched her head and got her hand caught in the sticky threads still caught in the back of her hair. She had to find a way to get that last bit of net released. She smiled and dug out another net in its small cover.

She pitched the net up as hard as she could and watched it cling to one side of the opening above her in the cave. Next, she gathered some dirt and covered her head so that the strands of her hair would not stick to her hands. Now came the hard part. She began to throw dirt on a portion of the net that was hanging down, to make a section to let her cling to it. Her hope was that she could cover a section of the net with dirt so that she could cling to it and it wouldn't be sticky, it would have dirt on it and protect her hands.

Tossing up dirt until she was tired, Brenna next lay down in the dirt and scooted into the deepest piles of dust she could find. Before she left the floor, she put handfuls of dust into a couple of front pockets to give more cover for her gloves as she began to climb.

The first couple of steps upward went smooth, but then her weight pulled the net and strands wanted to do their job, she stopped and pulled dirt from a pocket and tossed it at strands before they stuck to her jacket. The dusty strands just slipped back, and she grabbed more of the net above her.

When she got to the top, she was glad she had thought of dirt as the area where the net clung to the opening was sticky and ready to wrap around her hands. Here she was, fifteen feet up and trying to throw dirt on a net that wanted to enfold her.

Brenna realized she had been too efficient in throwing the net over one side of the opening. She dug the last of the dirt from her pockets and still couldn't get up to the floor of the next tunnel and escape the net. Hanging there, she made the decision that she had to sacrifice one more jacket. Hanging and changing hands, Brenna was able to get out of the jacket and laid it over the last of the net.

She stood up on the floor of the upper tunnel; she found here there was also lighting. There were also many footprints and drag marks. Great. She was sure that Zander had moved up to this level to track the maniac and her father. Her dad had taught her never to doubt instincts.

The air in the tunnel was warm as it moved over her bare arms. She cradled her weapon in an alert manner and began to move forward. Again, even though she watched for traps, she felt sure that Zander had taken care of any threats.

Brenna was aware that the adrenalin was pumping through her veins, and she was fighting herself to hold herself back. She caught herself walking too fast and stopped. She started out slowly again, looking around and listening for sounds that shouldn't be in this tunnel.

She heard a soft noise around a corner and knew it was too large to be one of the rats that had found a ride to Mars with humans. Being too jumpy, to begin with, she went around the corner, looking down the rough-hewn walls.

Looking down at what seemed to be deeper dust on the floor in front of her, she carefully stepped forward. Brenna was four careful steps into the dust on the floor when she sprang the snare and ended up in the air. Her butt was down, and her nose was bumping her legs with her feet over her head, all in a tight ball.

This was an old net, not one of the sticky gripping new ones that would wrap around and tightened as a person resisted or moved. As she struggled to get to one of her knives, the hanging net began to swing.

Her stomach rolled and then she heard laughter. Twisting in the confined space, she got enough view over her shoulder to see a figure too tall to be the maniac.

"Dammit, Zander. Get me out of here before I cut your net to pieces."

He came around and put a hand on her ass to stop the net from moving back and forth. "The miners were smart. The rope has metal strands braided in the hemp. You won't be able to cut it with anything but a welding torch."

He moved out of her vision and then the net lowered until she was spread out on the floor, dust billowing all around her. Brenna kicked the rope net away and scrambled to her feet, clutching a knife.

"You set a trap?"

"Yes, a harmless one to catch anyone who might be in the area. I had hoped you would still be hanging around in a power cavern."

Stopping to look at him she was amazed. "You made a joke."

Chapter Eighteen

Getting past any explanations, Zander led her to where he had her father and the others. The others were a maniac tied up and hanging against a curved tunnel wall and a young girl who was sitting by Brenna's father.

Hian Gunva looked like he had gone through the wrong end of a battle and lost. The little girl sat beside the unconscious old man. Yes, for the first time she saw Hian Gunva as an old man. Brenna had not thought about the fact that her father was fifty-one years old when she had been born.

He had always seemed so vigorous and strong, facing life as if it always had to be conquered and he was the one to do the job. He never taught her a lesson he hadn't done himself first. He showed her each lesson, each move, the accuracy of every weapon.

Here lay an old human male, with some gray stubble on his chin and sunken eyes closed against the brittle skin over bony cheeks. How had she not seen him before they left for Earth to take on the contracts?

Kneeling down beside him, Brenna took his cold hand in hers and sighed. She looked at the child. "You are very brave. I need you to watch him for just a little while longer while I go up to arrange for our return home."

Getting to her feet, she went over to look at the insane man hanging on the wall. Like her father he was unconscious. Unlike her father, he still looked hearty and no more than about forty years of age. He was dirty and bruised, and there were rips in his clothes. He was a Caucasian Earthman who had led a rough life with a lot of old scars to prove his choices.

Turning, she looked at the Veldan leaning against some type of old equipment. He looked so casual with one ankle crossed over the other and an arm propped on the old composite material.

"Zander, I need to find an off ship suit and a way to get topside so that we can be picked up by someone who we can trust to get us safely back to Earth. Any suggestions on any part of this problem?"

Standing up, he nodded his head toward the other end of the tunnel. She crossed her fingers as she followed his long strides down the tunnel away from the wider place where her father and the child rested.

The tunnel turned, and some of the lights were out, making it hard to see all the details. It wasn't that the power was shut off it was that some of the light fixtures were damaged or not connected. Zander disappeared into an opening, and when she caught up with him, she found him standing in the middle of a storage room with a lot of dusty stuff.

Dust settling over the top of everything meant that this room had an opening to the topside. She went over and brushed the dust off the rounded cover of the helmet of an off ship suit. Other than shaking the suit out, she was all set to go topside.

There was a set of composite steps attached to one wall and above was a door hanging open that led to the inside of an airlock. The fact that the inside door was left open explained the light coating of dust on everything in the room.

She sneezed as she spoke. "Any ideas where we would be safe for an extraction?" "Marines."

"Umhmm. We should also go to the Marine Headquarters in Georgia. It is the government center for American Government. We could request that the senator meets us there to pick up his daughter. With the Marines all around us, we could ask for the Veldan Ambassador to meet to pick up the artifact. We could also ask a representative of the Choban Company to show up so they can pay us for you."

Zander looked up at the opening above. "You will have to go up on your own. None of these suits will fit me."

"No problem. I will request a utility station to take all of you off in a protected medic unit.

They can put a tube over the outside opening. I will need my backpack for my contact mic."

Brenna cleaned off a suit and started the process of putting it on while Zander went to retrieve her backpack. The suit was large, but she was a tall woman, and she only intended to wear it long enough to wait for the Marines. Her intention, since they were on Mars, was to contact a unit of the Space Marine Corps. All she could do was cross her fingers and hope that Zander's trust in that particular group paid off.

Zander returned with her pack, and after she had attached her floating ear bud, he helped her make sure the helmet was secured.

"You go up, and I will close the door behind you."

Nodding in her helmet, she started up the ladder. The small airlock above was made from the expensive metal. All metal was expensive on Mars and scavenged from leftover scrap.

Brenna was surprised when she got the topside door open. There was nothing above, no sheds or any of the standard protection composite round tents that were usually built over any such entrance to the lower tunnels. She was grateful that there were no dust storms on the clear ground with only large boulders.

Using her mic, she used the special signal with her communication unit that Zander said would get her through to SMC. She heard the conversation in the background as a person with a higher grade was quickly added to the mic.

"You say you have the Veldan called Zander who was with the SMC against the Trios on the second moon over planet U231Z42?"

Keeping her voice in an official mode, she answered. "Affirmative. He wishes to talk to his representative on Earth. If you take us and our other captive and the senator's daughter to the Marine Headquarters in Georgia, America we would appreciate your help."

There was static that worried Brenna; then she got part of the answer she wanted. "Tracker, we are sending down a Marine Portable Medic Unit to take on you and your people. We will get back to you as to where we will determine your destination."

"I am setting up a locator that you can tie in on to find us. There are no outside buildings, so a tube will have to be set up to take the injured out of the tunnels below."

Setting up the locator, Brenna went below to avoid the dust the small medic unit would kick up as it came into land. She felt the tremors on the ground as she stood inside the closed up airlock. At last, there was a banging on the top door. Since she still had an off ship suit on and the bottom door was closed, she opened the top door and looked up at a medic inside a tube. He had a cloth mask over his nose and mouth, but with the wrinkles around his eyes, he was smiling. There obviously was an atmosphere in the tube, and it filled the airlock.

She opened her helmet and banged on the bottom door. One beautiful set of blue, green eyes looked up at her after that door dropped down.

"I think your ride is here, Veldan." She nodded upward.

"Let me hand the child up, but they might want to send a gravity lift down for the tracker Mr.

Gunva. They also need to send down some MPs for the maniac who kidnapped the child." Suddenly the small space of the airlock was full of Marines. Several dropped down after

Zander and Brenna just pressed back into a corner. It was a short time and the girl, wrapped in a Marine's jacket, was passed from hand to hand up to the medic.

He pulled his mask off and the smile was there. "Hey, there sweetheart. Let's get you some milk and cookies."

Tears were glistening on her wet cheeks, but she did smile. She gulped and stuttered as she spoke. "What kind?"

As he climbed through the tube, he spoke in a soft voice. "We have all kinds, but I bet you like the same kind I like, chocolate."

The last she heard was a child's giggle.

Now there was a team coming up, pulling a catch net with special gloves that could handle the sticky strands. They were moving the kidnapper up as a prisoner without asking any questions and keeping him completely immovable.

Next two medics went down, and there was a long wait that caused Brenna to go down on a heel and look down into the tunnel. A couple of Marines were just waiting at the bottom of the ladder, and one looked up at her but didn't say anything.

Worried about her father, she was trying to decide if she should go down, when she saw an enclosed medical body shield float into view. She heard someone say, "head first" and saw a medic hurry up the steps to wait beside her in the airlock.

Her father's unconscious body, totally supported in a gravity-free cover, was pushed upward into the hands of the man beside her. He, in turn, guided it upward to a waiting medic who tilted it flat and floated it through the tube and into the medic ship.

Next up the ladder came Zander. He carried a small composite toolbox that he had evidently found in the tunnel. It was apparent that the Marines assumed the artifact was in that box. Brenna stood and first saw the bracelet still on the tall Veldan's wrist, and she looked up at his face.

Zander nodded at her and went up and through the tube. The last medic and the rest of the Marines came out of the tube.

"I think we need to close this entrance permanently and mark it with a warning. If you go on into the medic ship Miss, we can do our job."

"I have a gray backpack with an initial B on it. I need that as it has information in it vital to the reports needed to the completion of our two contracts."

The Marines looked at each other and then talked to someone on a closed mic.

"Okay, I have been given ten minutes to find your item. If I can't find it in that amount of time, we leave."

It was all she had, as she sat with her feet dangling down into the opening, feeling her heart thump in her chest. She refused to look at her inner wrist at her timepiece, as she knew the minutes were moving away. A Marine beside her tapped her shoulder, and she got up, knowing he wanted her to go up and use the tube to leave.

At that moment her backpack landed at her feet, as the Marine below was climbing to join her. She knew it would not be appropriate to kiss him, so she held out a hand and shook the one he extended. Taking only a moment, she dropped her helmet, pulled off the rest of the off ship suit and took her pack into the medic ship.

She was shown to a seat that was forward and away from her father and Zander. A medic came to her as she felt the small ship lift.

"You need to drink this. We have to help your body. You have been through a lot." It was the medic who smiled. With that smile she couldn't say no, so she took the cup and began to drink.

After the first large gulp, she stopped him. "Where are we?"

There was that smile again. He had a great bedside manner. "We are about to be picked up by our big ship. I think from there we will probably be taken to Marine Headquarters on Earth for a decision of what to do with all of you people and your personal contracts. I can't wait to find out how that turns out. I hope you let me know."

He stood up and moved a couple of steps away. It was at that point that Brenna herself was covered by the blood and body parts of the smiling medic. The air was leaking out through the small hole in the side of the ship above her head. Instinct had her reaching up for the breathing masks that the ship automatically discharged, floating freely through the aisles.

There was the tinny voice of the pilot. "Enemy fire. Hang on to anything. The main ship is scooping us up hard."

Brenna stayed in the bloody seat, the air mask over her head and tried not to think of the missing smile. Who the hell would shoot at the SMC? The pilot was right about the hard landing, as it felt more like a crash. There was air in the back of the big ship when the small medic ship rolled across the landing zone with the screech of metal.

Hanging onto the arms of her seat, Brenna heard all the items slamming around her in the cabin. She knew one of those items was that metal cup the smiling medic had given her. Damn, life wasn't fair. She talked to herself, and she hung on for one more tilt and then the little ship stopped.

Even on its side, the pilot got the back and two side doors open. Marines were everywhere, helping to pull everyone out and calling for additional medics.

As someone helped her to the ground, the call went out to a medic, but she assured them sadly that the blood was not hers. Someone went to the body left behind, but Brenna knew it was too late. Feeling the deck beneath her feet, she was aware of the shudder of the ship's big weapons firing at something or someone.

A corpsman gave her a damp towel and a clean shirt. Without being modest, she stripped and dropped the bloody garment, wiped her face and turned to indicate to a Marine she was ready. She followed him across the large landing pad that held several skip ships and had to hold on tight to some bars as they waited for an elevator.

They stood back as several Marines ran off the elevator and then entered it with several more that were going up. She said nothing, as Marines in a war did not need questions from an outsider. Looking down she saw that the knees of her pants were dotted with drying blood. She was just grateful for the clean shirt. The Marines got off before her guide indicated that they were ready, so she stepped back until the door opened again.

They turned sideways to allow the hurrying bodies pass until they reached a large conference room. Her guide stepped inside and indicated she should stand just to one side of the door and wait. It was obvious this was the command center.

Among the personnel in the multi-colored suits that changed color as they moved around the room, there was a short, stocky man with the build of a wrestler. This man did not look like a stuffy top echelon Marine General who sat around in a padded chair giving orders to underlings. This was a man who picked up a weapon and led the charge.

"Sir, there are three of the black ships. They are hard to see and are ghosts. We can't find what is being used to block our messages, no matter what frequency we use. We have sent out three unmanned drones and one live with a volunteer. So far, only one of the unmanned drones have been taken out; and we think it is because we are using the old ones. The one taken out was a new design."

The short man asked in a sharp voice, "Who designed the new one?" "Choban, Incorporated."

Several pairs of eyes turned to look at Brenna at her words. She shrugged and stepped forward. "It is one of the companies my father and I had a contract with. They wanted us to fail in our tracking."

"She's right. The whole thing was a setup, including sending them after me." It was Zander, leaning against a console with several floating screens behind his shoulders.

"Sir, we have a contact."

The short man turned with a frown and pointed at a large screen. A face covered in a face blur was on the big screen.

"Captain, we mean no harm to the Marines. We only want the persons picked up from Mars. Send them over and we will let your ship go."

An Aviation Warfare Tech waved at the General and pointed at a screen that was going into the red. Evidently, the General understood immediately even though Brenna didn't. She did realize it was bad news.

The General looked over at his Engineman and held up three fingers. Then he spoke aloud in a strong firm voice.

"Three, I am a General, not a Captain. Two, I don't deal with people that hide their faces and One, we are out of here." He brought his hand down, and everyone felt the strange pulse of a grabber motor catching a magnet string, and their outside world changed.

There was silence in the operations room and then the General spoke. "Anyone have any idea where we landed?"

Brenna watched as the General's well-trained Techs were busy working keyboards and floating screens and brains connected to star maps let the technicians find where they had landed. "Sir, we are in a new system. The thread we used to get here has already shifted. That's the good news."

The short man nodded. "You don't have to tell me the bad news. Okay, I'm going to take a walk over my ship to talk to any injured and see about damages. Miss Gunva, you have freedom of the ship, but you will probably want to see your father first. I will want a meeting with you in two hours for a briefing on your entire contracts, both yours and your father's."

The same Marine who had brought her into the room nodded at her, so she followed him through the large ship. After going down several floors and many turns through some narrow aisles, they came to the hospital floor.

Here the hallways were wide and the rooms large and open with moveable floating dividers that separated sections or beds. Small robots scanned patients and cleaning bots constantly sucked the floor and walls spotless.

There was so much floating in the air that Brenna ducked needlessly. Everything was preprogrammed to miss anything, but it was disconcerting. The medics and techs just ignored all the floating and moving objects. They were used to the items and had faith that all of the items would get out of their way as they moved to help a patient.

Her guide stopped at a solid screen inside one of the doors. Using the touch screen, he typed in her father's name and watched a map download to his handheld. He nodded at her, and they both followed the map. It was necessary as this whole place was a warren of isolation pockets, office sites, sections of beds and locations of meds. There even were places for bots to recharge.

The guide stopped and pushed away a screen that exposed her father. There was a med bot sitting on his chest, and he was still unconscious. Her guide brought over a chair for her.

"Here," he held out his handheld to her, "take this as you will need it when you get lost on the ship. We all get lost every couple of days. There are food stations on almost every level with two large cafeterias on one and five. Clothes are also available on five. I have marked the General's special office with a star so just follow the map. Remember he expects you to meet him and what he expects he gets or he is real unhappy. No one likes an unhappy General."

There was silence for a few seconds. "When we get back I feel sorry for those three black ships because the General won't wait for any court to decide their fate."

With those words, the marine was gone, and she was left in a modern hospital with her father. She reached for his hand, but the med bot immediately protruded a metal hand to grip her wrist.

"Your body contains contaminants. Please do not touch." The voice was female, but all in one tone.

Looking around Brenna spoke out loud. "I just want to find out what is wrong with my father."

The med bot answered a request. "Patient has three broken ribs and two strained ribs. Compression has injured the left lung. Vertebra five through seven have been compressed and are being reset. A severe concussion has been sustained to the left side of the skull. The left ankle is broken through both bones and the left foot crushed. Blood loss was severe."

Brenna just stared at the little round metal sphere sitting on her father's chest. She cleared her throat and asked the most important question. "What are you doing to repair him?"

She hoped she used the right words.

"I have been assigned to make this patient whole. I have administered blood to bring him complete and stable." From this point, the female voice without tones or emotions told a long list of items it had done to her father to see that he lived and got well. The med bot ended by explaining that due to the damage to the lung area, the patient was being kept in a healing coma.

"How long for the coma? I need to talk to my father. Sorry, I need to talk to the patient."

The med bot sent up a floating screen. "It depends on the healing powers of a patient. At least another twenty-four hours."

Getting up, Brenna decided she wasn't doing any good here. She would find some food and then go to make a report to the General and maybe learn something at the same time.

Chapter Nineteen

Brenna wondered how the Marines always got good food and great cooks. She ate a hot meal in one of the small food areas just watching all the alert warriors who were watching her.

She was grateful for the handheld because not only was the ship large, it was confusing and a maze. Even with the guide on the screen, she had to stop a Marine to ask and found out she was one floor below where she needed for the last leg of her hunt. She smiled, remembering she was supposed to be a tracker.

She was pleased when she made it to the General's cabin right on time. Although this was his working office and not the Operational Center, it still gave the General answers. There was not a wall space without a screen or map covering the metal sides. There were young personnel moving quietly back and forth updating information. They actually had their boots off, moving in their stocking feet.

The General's eyes met Brenna's, but he kept looking at what seemed to be star maps with streaks on the plates of the solid prints.

"Sir, the Veldan is familiar with the spacecraft. We can lock onto a magnetic string right here and be next to it in minutes. On the other hand, going home is going to be hit and miss. We need to grab a string and drop out and take a sighting and grab another. We need to grab short hops so that we make sure we are not going in the wrong direction or overshooting where we need to go. This is all unmapped territory. When we grabbed one to escape, our Engineer did the right thing and latched onto the first string immediately."

The General looked at her again. "Okay, everyone not working on my immediate assignments take a break. I need to talk to the tracker. Bring us both something to drink and make it strong."

A Marine brought in what looked like a container and several cups of real glass. No one took real glass into space, so it was an expensive composite of some type. The liquid was poured into three glasses, and as she sniffed, she smelled the wonderful strong smell of old whiskey. Wow.

A long arm reached over her shoulder to pick up the third glass, and there was another smell she recognized immediately. It also smelled great. It smelled like jungle and male.

Taking control of her reactions, she didn't move other than to bring the clear cup to her lips to let the heat of the drink wash new heat down her throat and clear away the heat from the Veldan standing behind her.

"Tell me your complete story. I need to understand what type of problem my Marines face." Brenna took another sip and set the cup down. If he had asked that question in any other way, she had a thousand ways to build a statement. Instead, his concern for his people made up her mind. She would make it simple and the truth. She began by telling him about being offered the two contracts.

"One was by the government of the Americas to retrieve the daughter of the senator. The other was to retrieve the artifact taken by the Veldan offered by Choban Incorporated. Choban then also put additional funds into the senator's cause."

She paused and took a needed drink of the warming liquor.

"Sir, I need to be completely honest. Something that I have been trained to avoid." Shrugging her shoulders she continued. "We got greedy. Looking back at the situation, I think someone knew us well enough to play on our greed. We thought about all those credits if we took on both contracts.

After I turned seventeen, my father and I always worked together as a team. Since he trained me, we thought alike in the field and always completed all contracts successfully.

Theoretically, one tracker with my experience and my extra supplies should have been able to take down one man and retrieve an unknown artifact. A pick-up was available. The other contract called for the retrieval of an insane man with very little supplies and to save a small child."

Zander pulled out a chair and sat down beside her with his cup. "I can add to this General. The contracts were meant to fail and wipe out the Gunva Trackers. The insane kidnapper was given unlimited supplies, including traps, nets, and weapons. He had night vision goggles, additional clothes along with food and water.

I found a long distance contact mic, so I think he had a means to escape eventually. Someone was helping him. The information given to the Marines and Gunva Trackers was incomplete." Zander pushed forward a thin info strip.

"This is what was given out with the contract, and obviously, it is incomplete. What I found at the scene when I took down the kidnapper tells a whole different story. The Marines and the medics' records at that site will confirm the additional armaments."

The General looked over at one of the workers who nodded and went to work getting info for the General.

"It is worse." Zander placed a hand on the table and let it change. Both Brenna and the General watched the hand grow and saw the skin change; the color becoming something dark and different. The hand was soon twice its size with claws on the end.

Pulling a knife, Zander slammed the point down onto his mutated hand hard, and the tip broke with a sharp noise to rattle onto the table.

"They sent a single tracker after one Veldan and didn't tell the Gunvas that the Veldan was a rare modifier that the Marines had borrowed in an agreement. There has never been proof that a modifier has been killed by an outside source, and the Wisoo have only captured one that an Earth woman helped.

Both contracts had such high credits to entice tons of trackers but were only given to the Gunvas. Both contracts were meant to fail and destroy the Gunvas."

The hand had returned to normal as a broken knife was left on the table next to a clear empty cup. Both the General and Brenna gulped down their drinks and added empty cups to the table.

Brenna understood that she and her father would be dead if it weren't for the Veldan who had made love to her and then turned into a full hero saving the trackers.

The General looked at the two people at the table across from him and asked the question. "Why? What did you and your father do to Choban?"

Shaking her head, she thought back over all the many contracts they had completed over the years. She couldn't think of anything because she didn't believe they had ever taken on a contract for that company. It just didn't make sense.

"Sir." One of the working Marines stepped forward and held out a couple of info strips. "I might be able to help. It is strange that the Gunva Trackers have not taken a contract for Choban. They have taken contracts that affect Choban."

Putting the indicated info strip into a slot, a floating screen popped up and there were three information contracts for Gunva that were highlighted.

The young Marine leaned over and pointed. "See on this one the CEO was crooked and his own company put out a contract to find someone to prove it. Gunva Trackers took on the contract and got surveillance material to prove him right in the middle of some dirty deals. He ran, and they stopped him and turned him over to DA for prosecution.

He was married to the daughter of one of the main stockholders of Choban."

The young man took a moment to scroll the screen and pointed to another contract, blowing it up large in the middle of the table. "This is a case of weapons smuggling and three contracts were awarded, one to the Gunvas. All three were successful and the smugglers were apprehended, but Gunvas were given a bonus when they were able to trap seven ships with weapons being loaded or about to be loaded. The Gunvas disabled the ships so they couldn't take off and called in backup. The ships were declared salvage and retrieved to a government yard for auction. Choban originally owned the ships. Choban, who claimed they knew nothing of the illegal use, put in a claim for the ships. It was refused in the court. That was an expensive loss, really big credits. It set the stock to make a big drop."

The General nodded. "Thanks. I don't think you have to go any further."

Suddenly the General had his hands on the table. "You know, I think the Gunva Trackers are going to cost the Choban a lot more money when we get back. First, we are going to take out those three black ships and they probably are worth a pretty penny.

Next, I am going to stand next to this young lady as she collects her two-point-five K credits from Choban. I am sure the Ambassador from Veld would also like to join in seeing that those two contracts are paid."

The General stood, and both Zander and Brenna also rose. "Have someone show Miss Gunva to a comfortable officer's bunk." With that, he motioned for Zander to sit and wait.

Her handheld blinked but didn't give information as to

bunk areas. Suddenly, there was a Marine in the doorway. "If you will come this way, please."

She followed through the up and down the maze, and her guide told her how lucky she was being put in officer's bunks. When they finally got to a long narrow, quiet hallway with closed doors, he stopped in front of one and swiped a card. He handed the card to Brenna.

"This is your bunk, Miss."

She smiled at him, took the card, and entered the small room. It had a very long bunk on one wall. In the back was a combination pull down desk and stool. At the present, it was up against the wall to allow entry into the compact bathroom. A shower, sink, and toilet that almost touched each item were all that was enclosed inside the stall. Built on the outside of that bath area were shelves that she knew Zander would have to duck to move through the room.

It was private and quiet and clean. There were hooks on the wall under the shelving, and she took off her dirty outer shirt and hung it on one. She was surprised to find her backpack on the end of the long bunk. She pulled out some clean clothes and slid sideways to the shower. She needed a long hot shower.

In her many contracts and hunts, she had put up with a lot less and there was a lot of hot water. She knew that this ship did a lot of recycling, so she didn't think about what the water was made up from, just that it was safe and clean and hot.

When she came out, she looked at her choice to wear. Her underwear was clean and useful, but everything else still had red dust in the creases.

There was a buzz, and a small white light came on beside her door. She grabbed a dusty shirt and pulled it on and then went to the door and pushed the button by the white light.

"Yes?"

"Ma'am, it's Private DeCow, your guide. Zander

suggested you would need clean items. I have brought you some things from the laundry."

Looking down at the long shirt that reached halfway down her thighs, Brenna shrugged, knowing this was a mixed sex crew and pushed the button that slid back the door.

It was her guide that she now had a name for, and he held out a military tote.

It was a standard one that had been used by the military for centuries with only a few modifications. It was bullet proof, weather resistant and had an anti-view protection and an anti-gravity mode when it became too heavy to carry.

"Anything else you need, just push two on the handheld I gave you and I will answer."

Brenna noticed he never lowered his eyes below her neck. Trained as a Marine to take care of VIPs. She found this thought interesting as the Private nodded and walked away. She wondered if he was part of a special group that traveled with General Richards. A man as important as the General would surround himself with special people that he felt he could trust.

The tote was full of two sets of everything, even PJs. There was one pair of comfortable shoes and one pair of high work boots. They were all in a dark blue solid color except for the shoes that were black. Everything was the right size, so she realized that she had been scanned somewhere along the way in this ship.

CHAPTER TWENTY

Having clean clothes and feeling relaxed after the shower, Brenna got a needed nap on the comfortable bunk. At the short buzz from her door, she looked at her watch buried in her wrist and found that she had slept for almost five hours.

She answered the door in bare feet and smiled at Private DeCow.

"Sorry to bother you, Miss, but General Richards has invited you to join him and the Veldan Zander for supper in the officer's mess. I will wait and escort you if that meets with your approval."

"Sure, give me a second to spray my mouth and put on shoes. Do you want to come in?" "Oh no, mam. That would not be right. I will wait right here. Take your time."

Letting the door slide shut, she thought about his statement that it would not be right for him to come into her cabin or bunk as they called it. Was it because she was a female, or some kind of a VIP, or maybe because she might be under arrest? She still wasn't sure about her status aboard this Marine spaceship.

She used the unit to clean her teeth and mouth, quickly relieved her bladder and squeezed out to the bunk to pull on her boots. She adjusted her long braid and pushed the button to open the door.

DeCow was standing in a relaxed but military pose, legs apart and hands behind his back, outside her door as if he were guarding it. He nodded without a smile, all business as he started down the narrow hall.

It was fifteen minutes before she began to smell food. They passed large rooms full of Marines who were eating or changing places. Finally, they got to smaller rooms, and Private DeCow stepped aside to indicate that Brenna should enter.

Stepping into the normal metal-walled room, she looked around the central table that held General Richards, several other officers, and Zander.

"Ah, the last of our guests is here. Miss Gunva, please have a seat." General nodded to a Marine who was working as a server who came over to offer her coffee. From the smell, it had to be the real item. She didn't care if anything else was served, she would be ready to drink a gallon of this black glory. Well, maybe she would add a touch of sugar.

Zander gave her a nod of his head from one side of the table. There was an officer sitting between them. Workers were busy setting plates in front of each of them, and Brenna realized she was really hungry. What was on the plate was food for fighting people, high in carbs and protein and all fresh and hot.

Okay, maybe food and great coffee would work.

Stuffing her mouth like the officers on both sides of her, she heard the General speak. "Lieutenant. Tell us about the spaceship out there."

The officer between her and Zander shifted and put down his utensil. "Sir, we are getting no response on any channel. We have tried pinging the hull and even hit it with a low range pulse weapon.

We do know it is hollow and has different sections near the hull as we moved around it. We can only get echoes in shallow results. We have found with the help of Veldan Zander two entrance points but believe we have identified three more that could be entered.

Perhaps Zander would be of help at this point as he has had personal experience with a similar space unit."

Losing her appetite, Brenna put her spork down to look at Zander's wrist. The thin golden bracelet was still there. It all fell into place. Zander had been with a group of Marines, protecting some scientists on a floating alien container, and found an artifact that belonged to the history of his planet.

She knew him, although they had only been together a short time. He claimed the item and felt it could be discussed with his own world's government. Probably the Marines agreed. If untold billions of miles away from Earth on an alien craft a Bible from Earth were found, the Marines would have claimed it to return it to Earth no matter what some silly scientist said.

She understood that this bracelet was older and more important than some book she was relating it to in her mind. It told an ancient story of the Veld world. It was important that the artifact is returned to Veld.

Zander also stopped eating, looking around the table. "My elders were contacted to have a modifier assist a unit of Marines to protect some scientist to enter an alien craft that seemed to be devoid of the builders." He took a long drink of his coffee and appeared to be considering how to continue.

"My first view of the alien ship as we approached, let me assume this one is identical. A Marine unit that also had a Veldan modifier attached and a Marine-Earth scientist were the first to enter that craft.

Their encounter left one of their men dead, and although the owners were either not on board or were dead, there were a lot of dangerous animals and killer robots still prowling the various levels of the craft."

He looked around at all the faces who were taking in each of his words. He allowed himself another drink of his refilled coffee then he continued.

"By the time I was volunteered by my elders . . . ," he smiled, and there were chuckles around the table, "it had been decided to investigate the craft with a better-prepared unit.

There were some scientists from Earth and two from some outposts. I joined the Marines for a briefing, and we were told to keep the scientists safe at all costs. We were also told we had a final word on all actions once we entered the craft.

It was determined that the craft was a collection or a collector. It was extremely dangerous to any living being. The owners had set traps and killer robots. Some of the items that had been collected were hungry beasts that ate anything and had a high degree of intelligence.

There were constant arguments between the scientists themselves and between the scientists and the Lieutenant heading up the group. They didn't like the fact that he insisted on a very slow insertion.

Fortunately, a small room was found full of shelves of small items. They were under protective locks that were difficult to open. While the scientist worked hard to open locks, one Marine just used a small charge and blew open one clear container. It worked, but the scientists were angry. Most went back to trying to coax locks to open while one scientist pulled items from the open container and started assessing them.

He couldn't identify most of the small articles, but made a big show of numbering and recording each artifact. A marine reached over his shoulder and picked up a rock. He told the scientist it was an uncut diamond.

The scientist announced loudly that an untrained grunt wouldn't know the difference from treasure or an alien gemstone. That went over well with the Lieutenant.

There were still a lot of the guys outside the door on alert, watching their scanners for danger, but at least one Marine had an idea for bait. I have to tell the truth. The only reason I began to look around was to give some support to the Marine with the rock.

I knew he was right. I have seen many of the raw and cut

stones termed diamonds. The scientist was an idiot. I walked past and was immediately pulled to something that was Veldan. As a modifier, my body is drawn to anything that can help me. I went over to the bank of locked containers and let one hand change; I used a claw to break the lock, and I took the artifact that was inside the container.

No one but me saw the artifact. The scientist asked me what I did, and I made a mistake and was honest and said I retrieved an item belonging to Veld. That led to a complete problem. I believe Earth people call it a fiasco."

There was a pause for Zander to again drink some coffee that a Marine was careful to make sure the cup was refreshed.

"Now with that long story, I am the only one here that has been inside of something that looks exactly like that ship bobbing out there in space. But don't overblow my knowledge.

We barely got one hundred yards inside that container. I have only repeated what the first team reported. I never saw an animal or a robot before I jumped ship with my world's artifact."

Finally, everyone began to eat again. Hot sweet rolls were being put on the table in several places with open plates of different condiments that looked like jams and butter.

Letting a Marine worker take her half full plate away, she reached for a large warm roll and spread red jam all over it. Brenna pulled her large refilled coffee cup in front of her and began to eat. She wouldn't have to talk with her mouth full, as she glanced sideways at a golden bracelet.

The General ate very little and only drank one cup of coffee. Brenna decided he was staying in shape, and he was a smart guy. The General's voice reached everyone as he spoke. He was looking at the officer next to Brenna.

"Lieutenant Dock, you will head up an insertion team. I want you to find the navigation station to see if they have anything that will tell us where we are located in relation to our home system." He looked around the table.

"You will need to take one of our engineers from the motor division and one of the Navigation Techs who knows what to look for when you find the right area. Pick the best four sharp-shooters and choose the best equipment we have to cover yourselves for off ship."

Now his sharp eyes dropped to her end of the table. "We have a Veldan modifier with some experience that will be necessary and one of the best-trained trackers from Earth. Docks, they will also need proper clothes and weapons. Get ready to transfer in two hours ship time."

Chapter Twenty-One

Brenna looked at the inside of the small skip ship as they moved slowly around the big alien container. The large round object soon blocked out their view of their own large ship as she looked across the shoulders of some Marines and out a porthole.

There were seven Marines and a tall Veldan with Brenna on this hunt. She had to wrap her mind around the project and classify it as a contract, a hunt, or she would question her sanity to be going into an alien ship just to search for navigation maps in a foreign language that might take all of them years to decipher.

From Zander's description from what was said by the first Marine unit, it was decided to enter from a point away from the large back section. According to Zander's description, this was a point away from the front of the ship and on the other container had a dividing wall that kept live captives away from one part of the ship.

Lieutenant Dock's unit had brought blasting equipment, but there did not turn out to be a need for that much destruction. Zander pointed out the door inset against the round end of the cylinder.

Their skilled pilot pulled up close and the co-pilot, in an off ship suit, attached a tube between the skip ship and the alien cylinder.

Zander led the way that didn't make the Marines happy, but he had knowledge about the entryway. He stopped in front of the inset door and pointed to the lit panel.

"These panels are all through the ship. Raise your hand to get the motion you want. Here it will be up to get the door to go up. If that doesn't work, swipe sideways to get it to move to the side. Remember these swipes as we travel. Also, get your sensitive nets out as there are trap wires that are invisible, but deadly."

Docks moved up and pulled out a spray can. "We think we have help on the invisible wires.

This is white spray paint used to spray letters on our own ship."

The idea of the spray paint was that it would mark the wire if it hit any and also mark their progress to allow them to follow their tracks back out.

Brenna was comfortable in the Marine clothing. It was a mottled color, but she knew it would change color to blend in with the background. The outfits were lightweight and easy to move in, but her backpack was heavy and the large weapon in her arms was something new. She was worried that there had been no time to practice with the larger pulse weapon with the grenade attachment and the lens that allowed her to see in a long distance and around corners without placing her face against the item.

Well, her father had taught her to adapt to the situation so that she would find the best use for this equipment. She found it disconcerting to be surrounded by the Marines. As a tracker, she needed to be up front next to Zander.

Watching Zander swipe and the door goes up, it was a surprise that they saw only black. From Zander's report about the previous intrusions on the other container, there was lots of power and lights on most levels.

Everyone turned on their shoulder lights, and they found they were in an airlock. It took only a moment to get everyone inside, close the outer door, and get the inner door to slide sideways. They were still in the dark as there was nothing but blackness beyond the airlock.

Dock gave an order for everyone to put on night vision goggles. For Brenna, she hit a switch on her weapon and let the lens show what her eyes couldn't see. She felt that if someone or something threw a bright light at them, she didn't want to be blind even for a second.

She heard Dock speak to Zander.

"Can you see any better than our goggles?" As they had put on the goggles, all the lights were pointed straight down to the floor, making a circle of light around their feet. They all had to keep their heads turned up away from the light.

She never heard Zander's answer to the Lieutenant.

For Brenna, her screen on her weapon showed a green view of what was up in the blackness above. All that showed was a metal ceiling that was very high above their heads. In the distance, the strange green outlines of pipes turned red that exposed hot pipes and probably electrical wiring beyond this short hallway.

Looking away from the screen she saw the thin layer of dust on the floor showing the footprints of the men with her. Beyond them, the dust was just a soft layer, smooth over the floor. As Zander and the men moved forward with their lights dim and pointed downward, she saw the end of the short hallway.

As the men's lights reached the end and beyond, she saw the difference. On the left side the dust continued, untouched and on the right past the turn, the floor was clean. There was no dust with no prints and no tracks.

Dock called a tech up. "Any life or sign of movement?"

The Marine held out a tablet and showed the negative report.

"What do you think, Zander? Ahead, left or right?" Dock waved away the tech. "Left," Brenna answered for Zander.

"The tracker is right." Zander turned to look at her.

But the Lieutenant had doubts. He was use to his trained personnel, and she was an outsider.

Brenna took a breath to hide her anger. "Take off your goggles and turn up your lights. Don't worry about alerting anyone. If we didn't let them know we were here when we came through the airlock, then we are very lucky."

A couple of Marines had already pulled up their goggles, and Dock lifted his heavy mixed-use goggles over his head. With the lights turned up and bringing all eyes to the floor, there were puzzled expressions on some faces.

Stepping forward, Brenna looked towards the left side of the wall past the end of the hallway.

There was about a four-foot wide clean path leading away from this starting point.

"Oh look, someone brought their home vac to tidy up the place. How thoughtful." She looked up at Zander who shook his head at her humor. She remembered that in all the times she knew him he had only told one joke. Evidently, shape shifters took a long time to learn to laugh. She looked around and added that even Marines did not get the funny bone passed to them either. This was going to be a dull hunt.

The Lieutenant did take a moment to swing his light around and then he made a firm decision. "Two shooters up one step behind the tracker and the Veldan and two on point six. Techs, we're looking for movement and power source."

They started down the left side of the wall. She heard Zander's low voice. "How recent do you think this was done?"

She looked down as she placed her boots on the metal. There was no new dust but over at the side, there were some small drifts from where the dust had not been removed or touched. "It had to be recent."

Sticking a finger in her mouth, she held up the moist digit and felt no air movement. "I don't feel the air, but still, dust moves and settles over time. More important is the question of why? Why would someone or something need to clean off a portion of the metal floor?"

Zander answered her thought. "To keep someone or something clean."

Behind them, Dock asked a question. "Do you think this proves that someone is still on this ship?"

At the same time Zander said, "Hard to tell," and Brenna whispered, "Probably."

Hearing both answers, the Lieutenant and a couple of his guys moved their larger lights around. It was at that point that the young Marine walking one step behind her and next to the dust on the outside of their trek, fell towards her, throwing blood over the bottom of her pants.

Chapter Twenty-Two

Brenna was so tired of having the blood of these brave Marines spread across her clothes.

Zander pushed Brenna back and down as he shut her light off. She heard Dock yell "Lights out" but the trained Marines had already begun to separate as they created darkness.

Not pushing him off of her, she placed her mouth near his ear. "Can you see him?" His breath tickled her cheek. "Three. Help me get my clothes off."

They had done this once in dim light, so while she heard the Marines move around with their goggles in place, she soon had a pile of extra clothes beside her as Zander moved away. Now she found a problem with the neat gadgets on her weapon. If she turned on the night vision view screen, it would glow and mark her position for any to spot in the dark around her.

As Zander was gone, she understood it was up to her to notify the Marines not to shoot at a big beast. She tapped her mic.

"Team, be careful. Zander is changing into his form." She was whispering into the unit attached to her ear. She almost jumped upright when someone touched her boot.

"Tracker, it's me, Lieutenant Dock. Did the Veldan spot an enemy." "Yes sir, he said three."

She heard the Lieutenant shuffle away. She heard some clicks and tried to remember the meaning of the codes. She heard shuffling but felt it was better to stay against the wall. Somewhere down in her backpack was her set of goggles.

Maybe it would be smart to dig them out when things settled down.

In the ear bud, the Lieutenant spoke. "Anyone got sight? How about long distance, Tech?" The Tech answered, "Negative, Sir."

"Okay." It was the Lieutenant. "Tracker, any idea which direction the Veldan went?"

Brenna was still against the wall where Zander had pushed her with the first noise. She answered in a low voice. "Anyone see tracks in the dust before the lights when out? Can anyone see any with the night vision? If not, Zander took the clean path." She hesitated and then had to add. "Remember he is in his modified form. Don't shoot the wrong stranger."

The men were up and organized with the Lieutenant and the tracker in front. She had on goggles that let her see a world in shadows of greens and pale reds. Shadows moved in and out, but the glasses made the blackness have dimensions, and she could see depth as they moved down into a large area with some kind of consoles.

With the Lieutenant holding up a fist, everyone froze including Brenna. Silently he pointed at two men and swung his fingers at a large long box-like form. Two Marines moved out. They were now down two men, the one who had been killed and one who was standing guard over the body and watching the exit point.

With Dock sending two over and down behind the box-like item outlined in the dark, this left her and the Lieutenant with two other Marines. He was leading them into a different direction to another box-like the console when they all froze again as they saw movement against the far wall. A door was sliding upward.

Dock looked over at the two Marines that were closer to the opening door. He raised three fingers and began to count down. When the last finger folded down, the two Marines raised up over their shelter and fired with their goggles letting them see a red body at the door. The red separated into two figures as one went down on the floor with the second pulling back behind the wall and disappearing.

For Brenna, there was a clear breath as neither blurred red figure was large enough to be Zander in his modified form. Neither was tall enough to be Zander in his normal form.

Dock was talking on his mic on a different frequency, but Brenna was close enough to hear.

He was calling in a backup unit and a pick-up for the dead marine at the exit point.

Suddenly he was talking to her, face to face, not through a mic. "Tracker, is this the Command Center or Navigation Point of this ship?"

Looking at the layout of the consoles, she knew they were workstations. "No. This is a work or monitoring area. We need to go up. Zander had probably already headed in that direction. We have to hope these marauders haven't done any damage."

"Wait." Dock got over and right in her face. "You don't think these short people that are shooting at us own this ship?"

"No Sir. If they owned this container they would have it powered up and ready to travel. These are pirates or thieves. I have a feeling if we had come in that back door we would have found their ship inside that large landing door.

They have some basic knowledge of this ship, but not enough to be able to move it. They are here to take some things and move on. We have interrupted them. I need to look at the one down in the doorway. The body will tell us a lot."

Through the mic, Dock gave an order. "Spread out and secure the room. We need that body.

Nav. Tech, can you tell me anything about this area?"

"Not much, Sir. Without light, I can't confirm a lot, but it looks like just a work area. It's a guess because you can never tell what an alien mind designs in its ships."

"So where is the fuckin' Control Room?"

There was silence to the Lieutenant's demand. Then he added. "Who has the door with the enemy outside?"

There were two clicks and with her green and red views she saw men move up slowly to the side of the open door. Brenna sighed and knew what had to be done, and it wasn't her sitting here watching what was happening. She pulled out a small flash bomb and a net bomb.

Working her way up behind the Marines, she yelled. "Cover your eyes." Even before her words, she was throwing the flash bomb followed by the net on the opposite side of the door from where the figure had first disappeared.

She had a hand over her goggles knowing what would happen when the metal ball bounced in the hallway. She still saw her fingers outlined from the flash and a yell from whatever had found a way to move to the other side of the opening. The fact that it was fighting the sticky net proved that her options had proven the correct way to move.

She felt heavy hands pulling her back as she was thrown down on the floor. Someone turned on one light, very dim, shining it at the body that was killed in the doorway.

A couple of Marines carefully eased around the doorway and stopped. One reported.

"Hey LT. The tracker has a live one in a net."

There was complete silence and no movement for a moment except for the struggles outside the door.

Dock sighed. "What the hell was that all about, Tracker?"

Still snow blind with her goggles on, she stayed down and answered. "Just doing my job. We all saw two figures when the door opened. Your shooters got one immediately. I figured the other was still around, but he would try to be sneaky. Since it is dark in here, they either see in the dark or have enhancements like we do. I decided what I would do and knew he had moved to the other side. I took care of it. Like I said, just doing my job."

She heard a grunt from someone, and as her eyesight was coming in behind the goggles, she saw the Lieutenant sitting on a heel beside her.

"Okay team. We have control of this room. Bring in the dead guy and someone figure out how to reach out and drag in our prisoner without exposing one of us. We will close that door. Perhaps we can chance some light and see what these guys look like and if they talk."

Brenna sat up. "Throw out a rope with a weight on the end. It will stick to the net, and you can drag him into the room."

Dock wasn't happy. "You know my men are Marines. They will be able to figure a few things out all by themselves."

Oops, someone stepped on someone's toes. She knew it wasn't a male/female thing, so it had to be a Marine thing. She just sat where she was and kept her mouth shut. She did hunt out some water for a quick drink. Her backpack was full because when she had first hunted out her goggles, she had tucked in Zander's clothes that had been sitting in a pile beside the wall when someone started shooting.

Working well together, the Marines got the dead body and the live one inside a sticky net, into the room. Someone swiped the panel at the side of the door, and they were in an area where they thought they might have control.

Dock was in full command mode. "One guy beside that door on full alert. Engineer Towbourgh, look around and see if anything in here is useful. Tracker, let's look at the enemy. I want everyone to keep the lights dim and pointed down unless you have a good reason."

The guy in the net had figured out that it was best not to move. A sticky net was manufactured to tighten on anything within its grasp and to continue to tighten if there was any struggling within its control.

The Lieutenant lit up the dead body first. Brenna knelt down and looked at the male close. She classified it as a male in her mind without checking for genitals. The clothing seemed to be a type of leather that had been closed with some type of bonding. It was very durable and would repel most dirt and protect from a lot of difficult atmospheres.

He had several knives on him that she pulled off. Two were hidden. "Lieutenant, watch the other one when it is released. I'm sure there are hidden knives and maybe a hidden weapon."

There were two kill zones. The Marines had shot solid bullets, one into the chest and one in the head. As she pulled the top piece of clothing apart, the body fluids that were a dark purple had stained everything. Brenna dug out safety gloves to protect her hands.

She found small items that didn't fit for a warrior. She began to put all of the items beside the knives on the floor. There were rusted bits of metal, folded items with writing, lots of round items that could be coinage from different civilizations and what looked like broken pieces of weapons.

Under his armpit, she did find a real weapon that looked like a small but deadly phaser. She held it up to Dock. "The other one will probably have one like this hidden on him somewhere."

She pulled out her multi-tool and cut off his boots and pants. His pants pockets held small chains and again lots of round items, including some colored balls. Brenna had an idea some of the colored balls were weapons. She put those on the other side of the knives and heard Dock hiss as she checked his genitals. He was male in a humanoid way, and he had another of the small weapons tucked in a clear holding device near the back of his buttocks.

Brenna leaned back on her heels and looked at the pile on

the floor. "Lieutenant, I can say with some surety that these people are pirates or private marauders."

Waving at the knives and the weapons on the floor, Brenna continued, "They are well armed in an individual manner. Their clothes are made from something I have never seen, yet the fabric is strong and durable for traveling in rough terrain. The fact that they were allowed to pick up prizes of their own . . . ," she pointed at the pile of junk beside the weapons, " . . . proves that they work together but are not organized like your Marines. They are a group of greedy males, probably without success on their own. Some leader with a ship has promised them wealth as they steal."

She stood up, taking off the protective gloves and looked around. "They are like us. Just stumbled across this big cylinder and decided to help themselves. We got in their way. On the other hand, they were more than ready to attack the owners if any were still on this ship. My guess is their morals are on a very low level, and we need to find that Control Center and get out of here ASAP."

Dock turned his light over on the enemy in the net. "Can we learn anything more from him?" "I don't think so. He is dangerous and if we let him loose he will warn his buddies. He will speak a language we don't have time to learn. I would suggest knocking him out and having someone from the back-up unit transport him back to the mother ship.

They can study him there in safety and find out what he might know about this container. At this point, we have no idea how many of these dwarfs are on this vessel."

"Dwarfs?" Dock flashed his light over at her and quickly pulled it away to look at the face of the alien with a hole in his head.

Shrugging, Brenna pointed at the dead body. "Stocky and with dark skin. He has a beard and no neck and broad shoulders. His legs are short, and his hips and belly are wide. He is right out of the old Earth fairy tales. Dwarf. Even his dark clothes look like leather, and he has lots of knives."

Brenna got up and moved over with Towbourgh and Chapton, the two Marines who had special training and were looking under the dust at the workstations.

The dust here was not very thick, so this area had been closed off and had some cleaning or filters available. She turned her light on and saw the clean track go out the door when the two dwarfs had attacked the Marines.

Not using a mic, she heard a man speak. "Hey boss, can I knock this dwarf out? I have my pulse on low beam."

A smile touched her lips as she realized the name was going to stick to these alien thieves. She stopped to wonder where her beast was at this moment. Brenna was worried about Zander. He was just so sure about his invincibility, but she had to believe the modifiers could be killed, like dumping them into space.

Unfortunately, in his modified form he couldn't use an ear bud or talk to anyone. He could make clicks on a mic if he got his large claws on one. If he changes forms, he would be left naked and without weapons. He had some talents in his normal forms such as the ability to see in the dark and more strength than an Earthman of his size. But unlike his modified form, any weapon could injure or kill him.

Brenna had to admit she didn't like the beast side of Zander, but she was hoping in her heart that inside this dark alien cylinder that he was staying in that form to be safe. She wanted him to return and make it soon.

Dock came over to ask his two techs if they had discovered anything useful. It was at that moment that she heard words coming through on his mic.

"This is Unit B. We are under combatant fire at the entrance point. We have extracted inactive Marine and taken one wounded out. We are setting up movable barricades to protect. Mother is sending in heavies."

"Listen up team." Dock's voice carried in the metal room. "Backup is slow and in a firefight. We will do what we were sent in for and advance upward. Leave the two enemy forms in this location, but make sure they are secure. Leave a locator for the backup team."

The Marines put the dead enemy into a body bag and hung both on a wall. The one in the net was unconscious and looked like he would stay that way for a long time.

"Okay Tracker, which way?" The Lieutenant stood by the open door to the dark area. This was too good to miss. "Follow the yellow brick road."

There was silence. Geez, Marines had no sense of humor. "Take the path that is clean." Someone turned their light into the darkness and saw the clean path near the wall outside the door.

Someone mumbled that they wished they knew what the hell was sweeping the metal floor. Brenna also had that wish. For one thing, the floor was too clean. If something was just being dragged across the floor, it seemed like there would be streaks and some dust left behind in some areas. This was a pristine, down to the metal and no dust left on the metal floor. Aunt Ethel had come in with a wide broom and a mop and cleaned twice. That went through Brenna's mind, but she remembered the frown on Dock's face, so she kept it in her mind.

She let a couple of Marines take the lead and spent time with the lights out looking at the strange colors with the goggles in place. This area had large piles of some type of containers and boxy types of receptacles.

What bothered her instinct as a tracker knew that there were just too many places for others to hide. There were too many aisles that were perfect for a surprise assault. One of these Marines could be picked off with a single shot by a sniper.

She was walking with her back to the wall, waiting for the first sign of movement. She saw the flash before she could push anyone out of the way, but she did yell as she ducked and fired her own heavy weapon.

Chapter Twenty-Three

Evidently, she wasn't the only one watching away from the wall. Someone else had fired a wide beam pulse weapon before her fast weapon let out its loud noise.

Brenna's eyes were blinded through her goggles, but the green sight came back, and a red outlined figure showed lying across a flat surface off to the side. She looked ahead as the men looked at the dead target and saw another red movement. She tapped a man next to her and pointed out with a nice warm red finger.

The Marine glanced at her and then off to where she was pointing and without hesitation, he fired his weapon. A red outlined figure fell down between some containers.

At this point, she heard Dock's terse order. "Hold. Anyone see anything? Tracker?"

No one said anything, so Brenna decided to keep her mouth shut. She decided he only wanted a report on sightings. In her ear bud, she heard someone mutter.

"I'm not breaking our small group up to check on those two. The one has not moved, and the other is either dead or injured. I believe the Tracker saw them first." He moved to where he was standing above her. She thought he was making a target of himself, and she could stand up as he was between her and any shooters.

He spoke directly to her and not through the mic. His voice was almost a whisper, so his men were not included in this conversation. "You guessed where they would be. How did you know?"

"It is what I would do. I would get ahead and lay a trap and wait." Brenna waited for the Lieutenant's reaction.

Now Dock turned and moved to lean against the wall beside her so he could scan the containers. He turned his head to look forward. "Chapton, join me. Team gives us protection.

The Lieutenant put a hand on Brenna's shoulder and pushed her downward as he took to a heel. Chapton also kneeled on one heel and the team had their backs to the three of them.

"Tracker, do you think there are many more of these things waiting to take us out ahead of us?"

Brenna thought about what she had seen. Zander had to be ahead of them. She also had made up her mind that the ship the dwarfs had come in on wasn't as big as the Marine's mother ship.

"I think we took out the trash."

Both Dock and Chapton looked at her as if she had lost her mind. She pulled up her glasses to her forehead to look down at the scan on her weapon. It could see for a wider distance, and there were only the five bodies around her showing on the screen. She felt disappointment as she would have liked to see the beast's large form register on that green and blue screen.

Dock huffed. "Speak like a Marine."

"Looey, you need to relax and get some humor. It will make your life easier." She turned her weapon to show him her screen. "My gut says they only have so many bodies to throw away. They are probably loading their ship right now with bigger things they consider important. The boss sent these dwarfs here to delay us and keep us from going to the back of this ship and interfering with their thieving.

We need to get up to our goal and then get out of here before more noisy neighbors show up. Someone more dangerous than these short guys could be the next aliens interested in this container."

He looked at her for a long moment and then over at the Navigation Tech. "Chappy, do you really think we can get pertinent information from this ship?"

Evidently Chappy was a nickname for the Navigation Tech. She watched him carefully, trying to get a read on the tech's face in this darkness.

"Sir, I am here because there is a chance we can get home faster. Without a direct route, we can be grabbing threads that might take us years to get back to our system. If there is any hint on this ship that drives it, we need to get our hands on that information."

"That's it." Brenna clapped her hands and startled both men. The trained Marines did not turn around, just kept their weapons pointed out on alert.

"Dammit' Tracker, I'm tired of your shit. You are good; I admit that, but you need to share and not in kids words."

Brenna nodded. "Think, what is in our control room."

The Lieutenant shrugged. The tech was smart enough to keep quiet. "I'm serious, Lieutenant. What is in the control room?"

Dock's frown was hard to see in the reflection of her screen. "Screens, read outs, the Captain's chair and controls for steering the ship. What are you getting at Tracker?"

Now the Navigator Tech found his balls and spoke. "The information is fed up to that room from various places on the ship. The engine room, the nav room, the sensing or x-ray room, various points throughout the ship including the landing bay and the entire outside skin."

Brenna waited, watching the reflections on Dock's face. The Lieutenant was a good Marine, through and through. But she believed he was also a very intelligent man with good instincts. Both she and the tech gave him time to work it out in his head.

"Chappy, where is the nav room?"

The tech shifted on his heels. "On our ship, there are two obvious places. One is what we call the nav lab. It looks like a workroom similar to the one here that we just left. The other is close to the engines."

Brenna turned her weapon so both of them could see her screen. "I vote we go to the engine room. Even if we find the right workroom, we don't speak or read the language. In the engine room, our Engineer and Chappy here have a good chance of recognizing something even if they can't read the instructions."

"Okay, Tracker. Any guesses where the engines for this tube might be located?"

"You aren't going to like it, but I guess it would be below where that big door is that we saw when the cylinder was checked."

Dock shook his head. "You mean the big door that you think the pirate ship might have entered and where they might still be hiding? Fuck."

The metal under their feet shuddered.

There was a firm nod from the Lieutenant. "The boss let loose a heavy pulse. I guess that took care of the ones harassing Unit B."

Gathering his men, he gave instructions to Unit B on where to pick up the bodies of the two dwarfs. No one said anything about using the new ID for the aliens shooting at them.

Talking to Unit B, the Lieutenant added some information. "We are going to look for the central stairway that was in the first report. There is some strong indication that the grab info we need will be within the engine area. That also means we will run into invisible wires and more dwarfs. We will keep reporting as we go. We are missing the Veldan."

The decision of the Lieutenant was that the Tracker and one shooter would lead off. Her weapon's scanner was able to see further with a more reliable output. They also could use some of their own flashlights without interfering with her scan.

Someone reminded her to make sure she had her spray can of white paint available. Brenna was not worried about being in front; it would have been her choice all along. The Marines had a pecking order of who was in front and Zander had a protective internal mentor. As a result, normally she was in the middle of the pack of this particular group.

She let the shooter do the alert watch ahead as he led, as she watched her scanner on her weapon. It showed the deep shadows between the green outlines of boxes and containers, but no living red glows.

Guessing that an hour of safe movement had gone by when the shooter leading slowed down. "Tracker, what does your scanner see in front of us?"

She changed the position of her screen. "Dead end. Let's hope we find a door that gets us into the stairwell."

Chapter Twenty-Four

Luck was not something that Brenna put much faith in, but the end of this wall with the clean floor answered several questions.

One, there was a door with a palm plate that let the door slide sideways. Two, they found their first invisible wire just off the landing. They didn't need white paint from a spray can. Three, there was a massive ugly slug cut in half on the landing and steps below.

With a lot of flashlights illuminating the stairwell, Brenna was down next to the part of the slug that was still on the landing. Her scanner on her weapon did show a faint outline in red with some green and fading red around the ugly hump. It was either dead and cooling or just dying slowly.

There were some strange slips of gray skin hanging freely in the air, held up by something that her eyes couldn't see or recognize. Finally, someone sprayed white paint, and there was a tiny white line across the top step. Also, several steps were white along with a part of this ugly fat mass of gray pieces were also white.

"Well Lieutenant, we can tell the sci lab guys that the spray works, that will get a chuckle from engineering."

"Tracker, what is this thing?" Dock was standing above her as she punched at the rear end of the slug.

Brenna stood up. She was tall for an Earth woman, but among these Marines, she fit in nicely. She would march beside this fighting man, but she wouldn't take his orders. She was a free hired Hunter and only with them because of her skills, skills as good as or better than theirs. "It is what it appears to be, an abomination. It is useless. A giant slug that is looking for

things to eat as it moves across the floor sweeping up anything that will fit into its wide suckers. It cleaned the dust hoping to find mites and leftovers from whoever might have walked through these halls. There is no danger from it unless it happens to latch onto your foot."

Someone asked a pertinent question. "Is it dead?"

Shrugging, Brenna nudged it with her foot. "It is dying. It doesn't have a brain or a central system, so it is taking a long time to realize it has been killed."

She moved around it, stooped low and stepped down under the white wire. Not to be outdone, the Marines hurried down the steps in the same manner. One in front, letting loose short bursts of white paint.

They went down the steps that doubled back a level when suddenly the white paint hung in the air. Everyone froze, and the lead Marine sprayed across the entire step to show a long white wire stretching from side to side. Their lights also indicated that there was an inset door on the inner wall. They ignored the door, ducked under the wire and decided they had a map of the stairwell.

It took one twist back to reach another level that showed a door on the inner wall and a large opening to a deep blackness that they chose to ignore. They still stayed on alert, using a spray burst every step or two ahead of them to avoid a tragic accident.

They learned the lesson when a couple of floors down they found an invisible wire by the fact of a dwarf cut in two on a landing and steps below.

They took a moment as the Tracker and one Marine stripped away some weapons from the body that was cut in half just above the waist. Someone used paint to cover a wire, and they continued down, have the reminder that the wires were deadly, and the enemy is still around them.

It was several levels down and many white wires when they came to a landing that was larger than any of the others. It also didn't have an invisible protective wire.

They came down the steps in their usual alert and slow movements. A Marine with a spray can out was in the lead when they saw lights in the distance in the room off to the side of the opening away from the wall.

The Lieutenant had his tight fist up, and everyone was frozen. He pointed a finger at the Marine with the spray can indicating the man should continue. This was the first landing with an opening away from the wall that didn't seem to have a killer wire. The Marines wanted to make sure they didn't just miss it in this dark area.

It didn't take long to have white streaks all over the wall, additional steps and the wide floor of this unusual landing.

"Tracker, what does your scan show over by the lights?" Dock was asking for information.

Brenna changed the setting on the scanner, but nothing came in clear. Whatever was out there was too far away, and there was a lot of equipment on the floor. "My guess is that the thing with the lights is the dwarfs ship. I can't make out any details, and I don't see any movement. I get no reading of anything close. I am getting an energy reading to our left behind the wall. It might be where the engines are located."

He held up some fingers. "Shooters, can you see anything through your gun sights?"

One was lying down on his stomach on the white streaked metal floor. "Sir, that is a ship of some kind. There is one thing that is moving and sitting on the lip of it, great big legs dangling over the edge. That is probably the big boss of those little dwarfs."

Dock worked his body to the edge of the opening to get a

look in both directions. "Here's the plan. The Tracker, Chappy, and Towbourgh will go left, close to the wall to see if they can check out the energy source. I will go with my two shooters to the right and try to circle to get in closer to that ship.

We will call up a report to the General, and they can move a couple of skip ships to this entrance."

Chappy led the way with Brenna right behind him and Towbourgh on her heels. She had her scanner on, changing the settings to get any readings on living beings or the energy source. Towbourgh also had some energy seeker out and was following signals.

The three of them soon passed into dark shadows and the large equipment around them blocked out the distant lights from the ship or whatever it was that sat in the hold. They had probably moved into the dark shadows for about fifteen minutes when they got a click on their ear buds.

"Are you guys hearing us okay?"

"Affirmative." That was Chappy who answered. "We can't reach Unit B or the ship. How about you?"

She could see just enough to watch both men moving their arms and their mouths. Chappy was the one to answer. "Negative boss. We get no contact."

The reply was terse. "Be on alert."

Their equipment finally told them they had to move away from the wall and into the dark shadows of the equipment to stay on the initiator of the energy.

Deep in equipment too large to understand, Engineer Towbourgh whispered. "These are the tops of engines."

Checking her weapon's scanner to make sure there was no warm body nearby, she looked up at the strange built item looming above them. "If this is the top, I hate to think what the entire engine looks like."

Both Chappy and Towbourgh were working over a panel

that slid up to reveal what looked like a flat area that was covered with tiny small panels. Brenna decided that she was the protection while the two nerds did their job.

With her back to them, she heard her working male voices mumbling to each other in short words. "This one—Yes—How about this—Here—Got it." Brenna decided this must be strange tech talk and tried to block it out so that she could listen to anyone trying to sneak up on them.

One of the Marines tapped her shoulder. "Let's work around and see if we can help the Lieutenant."

Looking over her shoulder, she nodded. "Get anything?"

"Yep," Chappy answered. "Didn't you hear us say we got it? We need to get back to our mother ship with this information."

After all they went through, it surprised her that it was that easy. She was almost disappointed. But she wasn't surprised or disappointed in the two techs. They turned back into intensely trained Marines.

In full alert with weapons drawn and moving on silent boots, they began to creep around the large equipment to come up with the small ship from a different side than the one opposite of the Lieutenant.

It took them a long haul with hearts beating in their chests and efforts to keep their breathing unheard. As they got close to the reflections of the lights from the small ship, there was a click in their mics.

"Location?"

Towbourgh answered. "Sir, just west of you in sight of the target."

She wondered how Towbourgh decided what was west in this cylinder and where the Lieutenant could be at that moment. Marine speak was not something she fully understood.

"Report in. Situation is under control."

With that information, to her amazement, the two men

stood upright, slung their weapons over their shoulders and began striding toward the lights.

It took her a moment to get her mind into gear and catch up with the two Marines to approach the dwarf's ship. How had the Lieutenant and his men taken control of the ship so fast and without firing shots?

Chapter Twenty-Five

Walking several feet behind the two Marines, her view of everything was limited except the ship and what was sitting on the lip of the ship.

Zander's beast was on the edge of the ship, dangling his legs over the edge, waving his horrendous feet back and forth. As the two men in front of her turned to walk over to greet their teammates, she saw the floor littered with dwarfs. None of the short, stocky pirates were moving. It was obvious who had won this battle.

At this point, she could hear Dock talking to the Engineer. "Towbourgh, you have to find a way to get us in contact with the outside, either our skip ship or the mother ship. What do you need?"

Brenna lets the Marines work out their communication problems, as she approached the beast sitting on the small ship as if he claimed his prize.

Looking up, she spoke loud enough for the beast to hear her. "I suppose you need clothes when you change back." She pulled off her backpack and pulled out a shirt and pants.

"Sorry, the boots were too big to fit in, so this is all I could bring along."

The beast dropped off the edge of the ship as if a twenty-foot drop was only a step. Brenna turned to look at the Marines who were talking about a small door that was probably an airlock. The problem that she could see was at this point none of them had off ship suits.

By the time she looked back Zander was in what she called

normal form and closing the final clasps. She looked past him at the small ship.

"Did you do any damage to that thing?"

"Nope. Everyone was willing to come out and wrestle with me." Brenna lets out a huff. "I'll bet."

She walked around the ship and found a side door open. There was one short step, and she stood on it to look inside. It surprised her to find the interior clean without any comforts. There were some metal seats, open metal shelves with items on them and lots of hanging wires and tubing. She could see into the front of the ship.

Spaceships, planes, land vehicles, and water conveyances all had one thing in common. They had a front that a driver would sit or stay in to move the thing forward or wherever direction the driver wanted to go in the transporter.

Coming back around to Zander, she clicked her mic. "Hey, Looey. How about hitching a ride?"

"Damnit' Tracker. We are doing something important over here. We are trying to save your ass."

"Hmm. Okay, so maybe Zander and I will just climb into this little ship the dwarfs left for us and started it up and fly out of here. When we get outside, we will call the General and tell him to come around this side to save your ass."

"Fuck."

There was silence and then she saw the Marines all turn back to march in her direction. She decided she wanted to be up front on this little ship, probably with Chappy, so she turned, winked at Zander and entered the ship.

It was low and tight, but it would hold the entire group. Brenna felt it would put out full atmosphere since the dwarfs did not have help breathing the air in the cylinder. They breathed the same air like humans. Oh, don't forget it was the same air that Veldans used also.

She was going to bet her life on the fact that the ship would go on automatic to provide air for those who were safely locked within the sealed transport.

Dock stuck his head in, then gave an order for one of the shooters to check the ship out as he spoke to Brenna. "Tracker, if I can, when we return, I will bring you up on charges of nonconformance in all dangerous situations."

She looked over her shoulder and past the shooter. "You didn't think Zander had left anyone in here, did you?"

The shooter spoke. "Clear sir."

"Chappy, you go up front and see if you can figure out how to make this thing fly.

Towbourgh, how do we get the back of this cylinder to open to let us take this ship outside?"

Before Chappy could touch anything, Brenna had screens floating around in front of both of them.

Chappy yelled over his shoulder as the engines started. "Hey boss, get Towbourgh back in here. I think this ship knows how to get outside."

Without looking back, she heard the tussle as hands pulled on Towbourgh to get him in while the side door of the ship began closing.

"Hey Chapton, do we have air we can breathe?" "Affirmative, Lieutenant."

Brenna saw symbols that made sense even though she couldn't read the words. She punched a couple, and the ship began to rise in a wobbly way across the floor.

Chappy reached up and hit a screen, and the ship settled down to a smooth lift.

"Thanks." Brenna nodded as she continued to look at her choices. She hit the circle, and the ship turned in a circle, around two times before she stopped it facing out to the back door. She heard moans behind her.

Dock spoke in the mic. "Chapton, is everything under control?" "Aye, Aye, Sir."

Looking over at her Nav. Tech she smiled and put the finger on a glowing arrow.

He nodded but whispered. "You know if that back door doesn't open we will be into a flat work of art, right?"

Brenna nodded. "The builders of this cylinder had to have built in safety features. On the mother ship there are several safety features in the parking and exiting zone."

"Okay Chappy, you got the up and down arrows, and I have the left and right arrows. We will ignore the other four to keep it simple. I am going to give one push to the engines and pray." She yelled over her shoulder. "Everyone hold on."

Working together they got the ship at a fast speed heading to the back of the cylinder. Brenna didn't know if Chappy closed his eyes before they hit the wall, but she wanted to see as the ship slammed into the solid wall. What she saw was smoke.

The back wall turned into smoke, and the little ship slipped right through it into the black of space dotted with distant stars. She took a breath and then realized there was something important they had to do next.

"Chappy, contact the General and tell him not to shoot us out of the space. Tell him we are friendly."

"We are friendly, friendly. Confirm. Code zero red zero. Confirm friendly." "We hear you on ship unknown. Do you need help?"

Chapton looked over at Brenna. "Let's cut the engines and let them pull us in as that will be safer."

"Affirmative. We need a drag to shipboard."

By the time they were off the small ship and up in cabins to get a shower, Unit B was also back on board.

Brenna groaned as she looked at her bunk when an announcement was made that all members of boarding Unit A and B and those attached to the Units were to come to conference room 16 immediately.

Shit. That was all Brenna had to say to that as she stepped out in the narrow hallway to see Zander coming out of a sliding door across from hers.

Smiling she spoke. "Do you know your way through this metal maze to conference room 16?"

He nodded and reached out for her hand as he led the way down the narrow hallway. Marines and personnel ducked out of the way as he went through with his tall wide shoulders.

She just had to be mouthy. "Do you know if we are going to conference room 16 then there have to be fifteen others somewhere on this ship. Who the hell needs sixteen conference rooms on one ship, even a big one like this?"

They stopped before the elevator shaft and waited. When they got on to go up, Zander spoke. "Perhaps they have more than one meeting at the same time."

The door opened to another narrow hallway. She was on a tangent. "Of course. The toilet repairmen needed to meet; the laundry people needed to meet about the number of missing socks, and the wiring guys must meet to decide if they should change red to pink. The cooks need to meet because there are problems with equal amounts for the p&j. The paint guys want to put a brighter white in the spray cans, so that takes another room. The pilots . . ."

"We are here." Zander stopped before a wide door that led into a large room that was full of rows of seats facing the front of the room.

At the front, there was a podium and a table with some men already sitting down with a plain wall behind them. The room was full by the time they arrived, so they just took seats in the back and settled down to find out what this conference in room sixteen was about.

The General came in and went immediately to the podium.

"We have a lot to be grateful for due to a few brave souls. I am referring to the intrusion Unit A and B and also our guests the Veldan and the Tracker." He looked over the room and found her eyes and then went to Zander.

"We now feel we have some threads that will get us back to our home system in a very short time and our Navigation Department is working out the details.

We are also returning with new technology by the means of an alien ship residing in our docking bay that Engineering is studying as we travel."

He stopped and smiled. "They feel that since we got our hands on it first, we should have the first look at it and anything that might help SMC, especially my ship. They seem a little proprietorial."

He paused and waited for the chuckles to pass. "We also have one dead alien and one live alien to investigate. Our surgeons are doing an autopsy on the deceased to give us a report, and we have the prisoner unharmed and being studied by both physical and mental doctors. Perhaps we will be able to learn his language with some help with the communication devices we have on board."

He braced his hands on the podium as the ship grabbed a thread and moved instantly through space. They all felt the change.

"Yes, our grabber engines are pulling us closer to home. That brings us to an important matter.

We left because we were caught unprepared and in danger by three black ships that encircled us to attack. Those ships are still in our home planet system. We will not run from them again, and we will take them on and teach them the foolish lesson of attacking a Space Marine Corps ship.

For the next couple of days, we will take a couple of breaks between each thread and make some changes, putting up some special weapons that we have been asked to hold back by our superiors. We will have a couple of surprises that is not generally known, so that we can teach a lesson that will be talked about and discourage others who misjudge us.

I want everyone to work on any projects they can, but I also want full bellies and rested bodies. We need to be ready for war."

CHAPTER TWENTY-SIX

For three days that were sixteen hours long and between grabber thread breaks, everyone worked on the General's illegal ideas.

Zander was down in the Engine room doing heavy lifting along with their tackle for items that couldn't be reached by folding metal arms. In these places, men put magnets on their knees and arms and climbed as high as possible on bridges and then went up the walls like spiders.

Zander just leaped, carrying the end of some heavy cable or twisted metal rope up to where they needed the attachments to be finished.

There were men with floater units that could take them with the electronic equipment to bond metal to metal or other items. The General's outer ship was taking on a strange configuration as unusual ugly muzzles sprouted out from places and angles that were generally for a smooth exterior Earth spaceship.

The General's explanation was that this was the future. Even Engineering couldn't identify all of the weapons that they were attaching on the ship.

There were some departments that seemed pleased. The techs in the Science Department were running around like gutter rats with smiles on their faces and pushing floating screens into people's faces.

Brenna got to spend her time in the dwarf's ship going over the strange screens with both the Navigation techs and the terminal and mainframe techs learning the symbols. This led to learning some of the languages that they passed up to the doctors who were working with the prisoner.

They did tell the General they found additional weapons. He came to the ship, and Brenna was impressed. This man was a hands-on leader. That was the best kind because he understood what his Marines faced when he sent them into danger.

She was surprised when the workers around her let her explain what they had found. So she decided to be a Marine.

"Sir, the small round balls are explosives that can be controlled by these devices." She pointed to the colored balls and some squares with arrows printed on the squares. "With the same item you can have a small, medium or large explosion. We tried some outside. It is a good idea and works.

These are weapons like our pulse rifles, but ours are better. What we have that you might be interested in is attached to the ship. There are two cannons. They shoot solid missiles."

She saw no interest in the dark, intelligent eyes of the leader of these Marines, so she gave him the hammer.

"They will continue to penetrate as deep as you want and will explode when you decide. We only have six of the missiles and if we take one apart to learn the process behind them, we will only have five. The decision is yours."

He looked at the six long very large bullets coated in a blue color. "What controls them? Brenna pointed at the screen above the loading locks for the cannon. He nodded.

"You have done great work here, all the team and you too, Tracker. I know you have an intuition that out tops the schooling and training of many of my techs. Now I will make a decision and hope it is the right one.

This is new technology." He looked at the workers.

"We must take one to the lab so we can learn and reproduce them. If its cost turns out to be too much, we will pay the price. Thank you."

Their little show was over and they all got a good meal, and a return to their bunks. Brenna took a long hot shower and went across the hall to wait for Zander.

They slept together, too tired and in a different world of worry for sex. But they needed the comfort of being in each other's arms for a few hours in the ship's rotation period.

Brenna always went to the hospital section after waking to visit her father. The hospital corpsmen always found time to give her an update. Sometimes these personnel were women, but they all were called by the same title, left over from old Earth days when there were large Navy ships that plied the oceans.

The only thing that was now on Earth's oceans were pleasure ships that were licensed and controlled. The oceans were the only thing that Earth had protected before it outgrew and out used its world. The oceans were where Earth got its drinking water.

Hian Gunva looked healthy and flushed in the special bed that rotated his body and massaged it at the same time. Such things as bedsores and tired muscles were long gone from hospital units, as these amazing beds worked the body from toe to head to keep all blood and muscles in good shape.

A corpsman met her and explained they were going to prolong his healing coma until after the thread jumps. The doctors would evaluate him at that time and decide the next step in his healing process. It was also explained that this was normal, and she should not worry. Sure.

Brenna had her moment and went back to work in the small ship, using intuition over schooling. She finally pushed the right button on the star chart and found what she was sure was the home of the dwarfs. She called over a tech for confirmation, and they both sent the information to the right department on this amazing large ship that belonged to a General of the Space Marine Corps.

There was a klaxon sound that the General had ordered to be sounded to warn when a grabber jump was going to take place. This was especially important for anyone outside the ship or the personnel working high inside. It was a five minute warning.

Brenna used it as an excuse to sit down in the small metal chair and just throw her head back to relax. Finally, the five minutes passed, and there was that strange jolt that let her know the grabber engine found a thread and pulled them instantly from one place in the universe to another.

This left Einstein's theory intact and also avoided all the possible threats to a ship traveling across the universe in regular stellar time, such as asteroids, streaming explosions from star ruptures and the pull of black holes.

Brenna didn't understand the science behind the grabber engine and didn't want to learn it. She did know enough about the engines to be able to fix one if something damaged it while she traveled. But then she could fix a lot of things that she didn't understand the science behind the items.

There was an announcement throughout the ship from the General.

"We have four hours before our last jump. There is a chance we can land in the middle of the black ships. If we don't, our priority is to look for them and take them out. I want to give them a message that they messed with the wrong ship and the wrong people.

Finish your projects and go to your bunks. Get a last meal and get into fighting clothes. At the final klaxon be at your fighting stations. We are prepared."

She heard the stupid "Hoo-rah" yell all around her and realized she had joined in with the military shout. If this continued, she would be wearing one of those mottled blue uniforms that changed color to match the background. Geez.

Brenna left the small ship and went to her bunk. She had

finally learned her way through the maze to that location. Taking off the overalls that had been supplied by DeCow, she took a long hot shower and went into her backpack to dig out her own original clothes.

They had been cleaned here in the automatic ship's laundry, and it felt good to be in her dark green outer pants and top. She tied her boots, having hidden all her knives, ending with the last of the thirteen on the outside.

Giving up to not be connected to the Marines, she went ahead and put the military ear bud in place. She put on gloves and attached her heavy weapon, ready to go back to the small ship. Her job in this next phase was to take the little ship out and wait for targets.

The dwarf ship would not be alone outside the big ship, as the General was sending out several skip ships. They had been equipped with weapons, but their main purpose was to act as spies. They could evaluate location and damage done to the enemy.

Stopping by the first small cafeteria Brenna came to, she filled her pockets with easy to eat food and grabbed a couple of bottles of water. Around her, the Marines were also stocking up, but they were reaching for those high caffeine drinks and calorie loaded sweet food bars. Well, to each his own.

Chapter Twenty-Seven

The klaxon sounded, and Brenna was in the pilot's seat with Zander hunched down beside her.

She was surprised and pleased that he had decided to go out with her to fight this battle.

They felt the bump inside the dwarf's ship and then a couple of doors opened to allow the skip ships to exit. There was a downdraft flickering veil that one could see through that kept the air inside but allowed the exit and entry of the vehicles.

They were the third one to leave through the door on their side. It was an easy slide out into the darkness of space, and a familiar small sun star was shining off in the distance. They had come in on the outskirts of the system, just inside Neptune's orbit, but the big planet was in a rotation that put it away from their entry point.

They had this part of their home space all alone except for the locator markers that would let the satellites around Earth know that a large ship had entered the system.

Their own SMC ship sent a signal notice to SPC headquarters and all beacons so that they would be welcomed. It would also announce the importance of the command of this particular ship.

There was silence as the big ship used the local magnetics from the sun to move in this area.

The announcement was for everyone.

"Incoming. No markings and no beacon. No response on any frequency. Prepare to defend."

The ship came in fast with no lights and no rebounding signals. It was black and lost against the black of space except when it blocked any stars.

The General's ship continued to send out messages to the ship and on to Earth even as the black ship fired the first salvo. The messages to Earth would take some time to reach any of those satellites that were close to the home world. It would only serve as proof for later information.

Brenna saw the explosions as the big ship behind her was hit. Explosions in space are different than explosions in an atmosphere. They just form nice round balls. These also push in partial balls away from the side of the Marine's ship.

The explosions just keep expanding and dispersing until they get too thin to be seen. There were silent shots from the new big cannons on the side of the General's ship and the black ship tried to slip away. The black ship did move to miss some shots, but a couple of the blows caught it near the back.

The mic on Brenna's little ship clicked. "Tracker One, fire one pellet deep."

Looking over at Zander, she nodded and rolled the small ship over and approached the black ship from what she decided was its belly. She took one pass and fired a missile to go into the ship and bury itself into the hold of the black enemy.

A general announcement came in over her ship's speakers. She looked at Zander as she pulled the little ship away from the battle.

"Incoming. No markings and no beacon. No response on any frequency. Prepare to defend."

The lights and the markings on the General's Space Marine Corps ship made it available to see when she was close to it. The black ship, running without lights was something she had to track on one of the foreign screens to detect the large metal bulk.

The dark rusty color of her dwarf ship that had no outside

running lights made her impossible for anyone to see the small shape that wasn't big enough to blot out stars. There was a clear screen that could be opened in the front for the pilot to see as they moved, but it held no real use, so it was sealed shut.

Brenna and Zander got all their information from the floating screens and the boards with strange arrows. There was a large screen that had the shapes of the General's ship and the black ship. As the dwarf ship moved away, the two ships got small.

There were controls that could enlarge or change the positions of the outlines of both ships. Although neither of them could read the floating information, they knew the distance they were from the ships.

They wanted the dwarf ship to be far enough away in case they detonated that large missile sitting inside the black enemy. The mic clicked, and Brenna's eyes met Zander's.

"Tracker one. As soon as that second enemy gets in position, put a missile inside them. Hold on the detonation."

She swung up under the current black ship to hide and wait for the second enemy.

"The General is not messing around. I want to remember never to get on his bad side." Brenna spoke to Zander as she lined up some arrows to control the next bullet.

"He is a surprisingly honest man to have ended so high in the Marines. I am glad he has survived the politics that eat up most of the high officers from Earth." Zander was working to bring up the next incoming ship on a screen.

"You don't think much of my people."

Zander stopped and turned to look at her with what she called his blue and green eyes. "Lovely Earth female, I have had to change my mind a lot lately. I have found I have respect for some Marines in the field. They stepped up and protected my decision to take the artifact that belongs to my people. I am finding the man who is controlling that large ship has integrity and uprightness. I find my feelings for you runs deep, and I believe you are an excellent warrior.

But you are right about our future. I have no good feelings about Earth and could not live there, and I will not ask you to come to my planet of sand and jungles. We must find another direction."

With his interesting whispery voice done, he turned back to the front and brought up the third ship to compare with the other two for their comparisons.

The other ship moved away and took up a position to try to get across from the other side of the Marine ship. The pilots on the Marine ship swung the big craft swiftly with its heavy engines and put the second black ship below. The Marine ship moved away from both enemy ships, leaving them together, even though in space they were far apart.

Putting her little ship into full blast, she slipped away from the belly of the first one and her track took her over the second enemy in a fast movement going towards the large Marine's ship. As she barely cleared the second ship, like a tiny mosquito she dropped a missile into the side of the second ship that was turning to follow the Marine's ship.

Not sure how deep it went in or what it penetrated, she kept it on a second small screen right next to the first missile in the hold of the first enemy.

There were more of those strange silent bombardments, as the three ships fired at each other in a black and white glow of expanding and disappearing. Where the explosion could get some oxygen from leaks, there would be a flash of red or blue. The colors were sheltered for those two within the fast moving little ship as it twirled in whatever way it wanted to go.

There was no gravity to drag at the swift mosquito, and it quickly ducked behind the big mother ship.

Brenna reported in on the private communication channel. "Tell the General that Tracker One has laid the second egg."

Through her ship speaker, she heard the General give the final words to the two ships. The Marine's ship had pounded away at the two black ships, surprising them with larger weapons than had ever been brought to Earth ships. The first black ship was limping and the second was trying to stay at a distance that would delay time for additional help to arrive and keep the Marine's ship from getting to Earth.

Someone from the mother's ship communication room announced that there was the first blip of a distant ship. The third black ship was on its way, and the General was forced to act.

"Combatants, this is General Richards of the Space Marine Corps. I have had my communication unit climb into your systems so that all of your people can hear me on both your ships. There is buried on each of your ships a small bomb that will totally whip out your entire vessel.

Surrender and I will let you leave to be considered later in an Earth court." At the end of his words both ships fired together against his ship.

"Tracker One detonate your first missile."

There was no hesitation for Brenna. These were the people that set out to kill her and her father. She hit the button over the funny arrow over the missile tube, and her little ship had to move fast to put the mother ship between her and the explosion to prevent destruction from the debris flung into space of a ship flung apart into sharp little pieces.

She heard the General's voice as she fought to get the dwarf's ship into a safe position.

"You have ten minutes to evacuate your ship. Let the incoming ship know that they will be destroyed if they continue to approach. After we leave and make your ship inoperative, the next ship can pick up your lifeboats."

She heard the countdown coming from the communication room and adjusted the missile explosion down to the minimum. There had never been a chance to test these explosions. Brenna could only set the explosion to the second to the lowest burst and keep her fingers crossed.

The idea was that it would disable the ship, but not blow it apart like the first one. They would see if the people on board decided to run. Otherwise, she would set it back up to higher and have some more debris in this area if they decided to fight more.

The communication room announced that lifeboats were leaving the other ship. Brenna waited for the order to explode the missile, and just when it seemed like the General had changed his mind, the order came through.

She punched the arrow and waited. At last, she got the order to return to the big Marine's ship. Brenna took a long way around to enter the door to the landing area so she could get a look at the other black ship.

In this darkness, so far from the sun, she had to get close to see the ship that was on the screen. She opens the front window and both she and Zander stared in wonder at a ship that had been torn almost into two pieces. It looked like an egg that someone tried to crack, but it refused to separate as it stayed together on one part. It was just a giant crack, opened to the stars and letting small items float away from its interior.

By the time she and Zander got out of the little ship, they were surrounded and applauded by groups of hearty Marines.

General Richards walked through the crowd and held out a hand to both of them.

"We are in contact with headquarters on Earth. Tracker, your father will be taken to the hospital there, and it will be in Atlanta that you both will meet the representatives of our government and the Veldan ambassador.

It seems there are some problems with the Choban representatives, but don't worry. I have just been promised that the Gunva family will be paid in full for their two contracts.

Also, I have just received word that Zander is to return a special artifact to his home world. There is also some strange debris out here and the Marines are going to put up some safety warning beacons out to protect travelers."

CHAPTER TWENTY-EIGHT

Brenna was bringing her little ship with the name of Mosquito into the landing hold of the satellite rotating off the mining moon of Despo. Two years ago, when the courts had forced Choban. Inc. to pay off its debts to the Gunva Tracking Company, the courts had also allowed her to keep the little dwarf ship.

Her father didn't like to fly, so it was all hers, and it took her a full day to paint the picture of the bug and the name on the front of the strangely configured craft.

Walking across the floor of the inside landing area, she thought of all that had happened over the last two years. Choban had closed down, and its main officers were still in jail on one of the moons around one of the planets circling the home sun. Their assets had been sold and their debts paid.

This meant that her father got to retire to a new job. He now ran a true company called Gunva Tracking Universal. It took them months to get the paperwork settled and to officially move into the Gunva Satellite. During that time they had gone ahead and moved in and began renovations.

The hull was sound, as some scientist had lived on the platform up until the government moved them out and claimed the satellite for temporary docking.

The living quarters and meeting rooms were in a condition that could be used immediately. The cost was in the shipments of supplies to make the platform comfortable. Supplies had to be bought from places that produced them and then put on grabber ships to bring then in close to the Despo moon.

Next, they had to be transferred by skip ship to the platform. One of the first changes that the Gunva's made was to complete the docking systems that the government had started. With a couple of large outside docking rigs, big ships, even a grabber ship could tie up to the platform. There was an inside landing area for skip ships and her little dwarf vehicle.

What she had insisted be done next was to clear out the lab area and began to build a modern hospital. She had experienced what could be done in a limited space on the General's ship and knew that she had to allot enough funds to make this healing place state of the art.

There was also a section on another floor that had the walls removed and made a room for exercise and training. Then there had to be the armory. After all, they were trackers, going after the worst that this side of the universe could produce. The ones that someone was willing to pay to have caught, dead or alive.

Hian and Brenna also needed people. They needed help for their office and trackers in the field. It was important that the people be screened to eliminate sadists, spies and those that hoped to be trained to move on to become lone wolves.

They brought into their company an old friend who was an outfitter from Detroit. He brought up some office people and his sixteen-year-old daughter who refused to leave the office where Hian had set up his main location.

She was a pretty little thing, but more important she was a genius on the Matriarch. It was the floating place of information that seemed to know everything. This little girl kept them up to date on who was missing, who was paying for badasses, and researching the backgrounds on all entrants that applied for tracker jobs.

This pretty little girl named Patty was one reason that the Detroit provider was willing to become a partner of the

Gunva's. He only wants a small share of the stock and a safe place for his daughter.

Brenna nodded at a few people, as she walked through the metal halls to report in to her father. She had picked up some new rocker rifles and was anxious to try them out to find out if she could control one or if any of their five trackers were able to enact the controls.

The rifles didn't respond to everyone. It was a mental thing that required the operator to believe that they would work from the mind. It seemed that only four people out of ten could activate the rockers, but it was said that when they did operate, they were faster and better than any hand controlled weapon.

Patty, the little girl who helped Hian, popped her head out and grinned at Brenna. "No rest for the wicked. We have eleven recruits in the interview room, and your father is on a closed circuit line with the Marines."

Brenna sighed. This meant she had to do the first review. Anyone wanting to work for Gunva Tracking Universal had to fill out a long application form and pay their own way to bring it in person to the platform for their first interview. Unfortunately, the few that made it past the first interview hardly cleared the background checks along with the physical exams. Hundreds had applied, and they had only six trackers at this point.

She wondered where the honest ones got the money and had a hunch where the others got their tickets. The six that were working for them had interesting stories to tell as to how they got to the platform. Only one came from a rich family. The rest worked hard for every penny.

Wondering what stories these people would have to tell, she entered the interview room and turned on the cameras before moving to look at the men and women sitting behind the long tables.

There were five sitting at each table with the last extra male standing at the back of the room. A tall, handsome man with his arms crossed over a wide chest. He stared at her with beautiful green and blue eyes.

Two years of tears on her pillow, twenty-four months of an ache in her stomach, seven hundred twenty-four sleepless nights and here stood her heart.

She stammered and then found her words. "I am sorry folks, at this time we are not accepting any more applications. We have just filled our quota. We will pay your return tickets." She only looked at him as she spoke to the room. She heard the groans and low curses as she slowly walked out of the open door and leaned against the cool wall outside the room. Brenna moved further down the wall when Patty came down the hall.

"Brenna, you left the cameras running. I guess I will take this angry bunch to arrange for transportation. I also guess you don't want to tell me what happened." Patty raised her plucked eyebrows, and the pretty face just looked cute.

There was no answer to Patty's words as Brenna closed her eyes with her head tilted back on the wall. She stayed there, feeling like she was part of that metal as she heard Patty get the disgruntled applicants down the hallway with a promise of a meal.

How, after all this time, could she feel him as he closed in on her? Brenna kept her eyes closed while she felt the heat of his body as he moved up against her. Now she had to see him and opening her eyes with her head tilted; she was lost in his jungle. He took her to the planet she had never visited.

Parting her mouth to let out air, he immediately captured her lips. It was exactly what she remembered, heaven with all the stars in the galaxy swirling inside her blood.

Neither of them could say how long that one kiss lasted, but it did come to an end as he raised his head and looked down at his warrior.

For Brenna, she smiled and whispered. "You're here."

He nodded his head. "I couldn't live on Earth, and you couldn't live on Veld. But we could live on a platform. You have a choice to make right now. I have submitted my application; am I hired and is there a bunk on this satellite for my long legs?"

Reaching up, Brenna pulled her fingers across his lips and down his chin.

"I have a nice suite of rooms on this platform. There are a separate bathroom and a very large bed. It is lonely there since I am gone a lot of the time. Maybe your long legs would fit in it just right and keep it warm in the times we slip behind the dark shadow of the moon."

She gave a small grunt as he picked her up. "Which way?"

The End.

About the Author

I live in Florida and under the pen name of M. Garnet (Muriel Garnet Yantiss). I spend all my time writing, reading, or talking to writers and readers.

I write SciFi, Fantasy and Contemporary Mystery. Visit my web site at www.mgarnet.com to see other books I've written. I love to hear from you at mgarnet2@yahoo.com.

I answer all my emails and if you would be kind enough to drop a note where you got this book, it helps others decide what to read. This is a part of the stories of Veld and the shape shifters from that planet, so if you missed it, get the first story *Help The Beast* or the second *Forgive The Beast*.

www.ingramcontent.com/pod-product-compliance
Lightning Source LLC
LaVergne TN
LVHW050645100826
845148LV00011B/1990